HOLD THE REIN FREE

JUDY VAN DER VEER

Illustrated by

BERNARD GARBUTT

HOLD THE REIN FREE

Golden Gate Junior Books
San Carlos · California

To DORSA and SCOTT O'DELL
who insisted that this story be told

HOLD THE REIN FREE

1

IT WAS NOT the sort of thing a yearling filly would do; leave her pasture mates, fly over a fence and run behind her long shadow as fast as ever she could. A horse is a herd animal with small inclination to set forth alone.

What it was that started her off the filly didn't know. It must have had something to do with the early May morning, the sweetness of the grass, perhaps a wild, distant whinny half heard or not heard at all. She was going so fast that when she met a wire gate barring her way she couldn't possibly stop, and she cleared that too.

She slowed then, sniffed the grass, ate a mouthful of wild flowers, walked briskly on her long legs, snatched grass here and there. Her nostrils told her that there were other horses somewhere about and she stood still, lifted her head, and sent a long, clear whinny rippling into the morning.

She had a large white star on her forehead, otherwise her coat was a solid bay with shining coppery lights. She was tall and was going to be much taller; she had in her ancestry Irish Thoroughbreds. The destiny planned for her by man was to be shown as a hunter in the ring, to be sold somewhere, sometime, for a large sum of money, later to be a brood mare producing others of her kind.

Her immediate destiny came charging down the mountainside. Wild with excitement, she hurried toward the little band of horses. These were the Indian horses on the reservation and they looked beautiful because they were running free and now they were excited to see the strange young mare. Shining red sorrels, bays, brown, one black, and one red-and-white pinto—they were a ribbon of running color. Suddenly they all stopped to stare at the stranger and she stretched out her neck to sniff at the nearest. Both animals screamed, both struck out with quick fore hoofs, both turned to lash with hind hoofs. But this was not in anger. This was a way of expressing their wild feelings. Then they all ran, circling around and around, each trying to get near the filly, each wanting to sniff her shining coat, touch her soft nose.

Their hoofs made strong thudding sounds on the grassy earth, the crushed grass smelled of spring. They all cavorted until a colt, nearly a year older than the filly, stopped playing and began fighting all the others away. He tossed his tangle of forelock from his eyes, arched his neck, and lifted his hoofs high. He would have her believe he

4

was beautiful. Then his head shot out in a strangely snakelike fashion, his ears went flat back, he bared his short teeth. He began driving the filly, herding her away from the others, nipping at her flanks and screaming. She ran, darting to the left and the right, and then she swung around and faced him, reaching eagerly to touch his nose. He struck out with a fore hoof; there was more kicking, more screaming, until at last she would run from him no more.

Two horsemen approached, riding fast, shouting, waving ropes. "We get in trouble for sure if they find that mare here!" Driven in the direction of home, the filly didn't stop running. It was a fast race as the riders tried to turn back the little stallion, but the intensity of his instinct gave him the speed he needed. The riders should have roped the filly first, then caught the colt, but they had sighted the situation too unexpectedly, they had become too excited to plan. Now the ropes whistled near the heads of both animals and settled on neither.

The filly leaped the wire gate without a pause in her stride. The colt didn't clear it, tangled for an instant, but not long enough, went pounding after her with bloody scratches marring his coat.

The riders turned back. There was no use continuing the chase now; it would lead only to unpleasant discussion, to trouble.

The filly's arrival at the home ranch was not greeted with joy. Three people watched her come. One, the ranch owner, Carver Richie, swore. His hired man, a Mexican named Frank Lopez, merely shook his head in dismay, while Frank's boy, Kiko, stared with big brown eyes. "Run get my rope," his father told him. "Pronto!"

While a pastureful of yearlings came galloping to the fence to

5

look and whinny and show off, Frank roped the horse colt and snubbed him to a tree. "Catch Mia," he told the boy, "and put her back in pasture."

Of all the foals that spring when she had been born, Mia had been the liveliest, the most playful, the most curious. It was the hired man, Frank, who had first observed this particular bay filly to be unusually full of promise. He had nicknamed her Mia, which in Spanish means "mine."

Frank had lost no time in pointing out Mia's qualities to Carver Richie. Once the filly had been brought to his attention, Mr. Richie began to see in her what Frank saw, and the longer he looked at her the better he liked her. He began to feel that he owned a creature of great value, an animal in which he, as the breeder, could take utmost pride. He began to visualize a wall covered with blue ribbons, shelves full of trophies the mare was destined to win. In time, Mia might well bring glory to himself and the ranch.

Now, in one swift stroke, fate had cheated him, made a mockery of his dream. He turned disgustedly from contemplation of the colt that had given up fighting the rope and now stood tired and dejected. "Those Indians," Mr. Richie muttered to no one in particular. "Why would they let a thing like that run this long?"

His eyes fell on Kiko who, having caught Mia without difficulty and led her to pasture, had returned to stand beside his father. "Hey, you, boy!" Mr. Richie spoke so abruptly that Kiko jumped. "Get on that burro of yours and ride over to the reservation. Tell them to come get this colt before I kill him. And if I ever see him again, I will."

6

Kiko was hurrying away to obey orders when he heard Mr. Richie say to his father, "Frank, if the filly has a hard time foaling, destroy her. Anyway, we can't have her scrub colt on the place; we can't even sell it to somebody else. When the foal is born, shoot it. That's an order."

2

Except in irrigated pastures, the bright green grass gave way to the bright gold grass of early summer. Certain flowers faded, the hardy ones that blossom out of the dry earth took their place. The filly, Mia, settled down to grazing with the others her age. She was no longer in a mood to jump fences and gallop across the land. She did the usual racing and playing with her pasture mates, early in the morning and in the cool of the evening, but playing with the other yearlings triggered no impulse that sent her over a fence, as it had that morning when she had gone so fast she put the fence beneath her.

To the boy, Kiko, it seemed that she was quieter and somehow

8

friendlier than before. He spent time petting her, talking to her, looking into her brown eyes and wondering about her. Nearly all of Kiko's friends were animals because he played with no children his own age. Kiko and his father lived together in one of the bunk houses on the ranch.

Kiko had cousins who lived on the Indian reservation, that reservation to which the filly had galloped and found the mate that had met with such disapproval. Kiko's cousins were not allowed to come to play with him because Carver Richie, the ranch owner, didn't like Indian children. Kiko's mother had been an Indian girl from that very reservation, but Kiko could scarcely remember her she had been dead so long.

The only being beside his father that really belonged to Kiko was his old gray burro, Sancho. Kiko wished he had a dog but Mr. Richie didn't like dogs on the place. In the hay barns there were cats and kittens because Mr. Richie wanted them to catch mice. Sometimes Kiko played there and tried to tame young kittens that hid from him, but a pet cat would not have been much satisfaction for eventually it would be killed. Whenever the cat population rose to vast numbers Mr. Richie had a man with a gun reduce it.

By his fellow men Mr. Richie was considered a good businessman. He was very wealthy and to most people that meant that he was what was known as a "solid citizen." Kiko, however, had his own views about Mr. Richie. But, of course, what a half-breed Indian boy could possibly think about him would be of no importance to a man like Mr. Richie.

Besides his Irish hunters, Carver Richie had quarter horses and a big herd of beef cattle, all shining red with white faces. He even had

9

another ranch to which his hunters were sent for training, and he had a house in the city where he and his family lived most of the time. Other men worked on the ranch with Kiko's father and lived there with their wives and children. But those children were little more than babies and too young to play with Kiko.

Kiko, of course, knew more about the ranch and all the surrounding country than Mr. Richie or anyone else could possibly know. Kiko and Sancho wandered everywhere all summer long, down the long Black Horse Canyon to the south, outside the ranch fence, west to the rough shoulder of Black Horse Mountain. Kiko knew ancient brush-grown trails where only deer and coyotes had walked for years; he knew secret springs in the hills. Sometimes he played he was a prospector on the desert, sometimes he was a great Spanish explorer, sometimes he was an Indian scout. He knew to be aware of rattle-snakes and not to step near red ant nests. Otherwise there was nothing in the wilds for a boy and his burro to fear.

Occasionally he rode over to the reservation to play with his cousins. But not often. It is awkward to play with children whom you can never invite to your home to play.

September came, dusty and hot, with grass seared gray by the sun. The school bus came as far as the reservation gate, loaded, and Kiko caught it as it went by the ranch. When school first started all the children, cross and frustrated by their new loss of freedom, did a great deal of quarreling with one another on the bus. But as time went on everybody settled down and grew accustomed to the routine.

That year the first rains came in November and soon after the earth was lifting and cracking with the strength of the new grass. There was one snow in December and one snow in February and rain between times. By March it looked as if there was going to be a good grassy spring. And the filly, Mia, still looking too leggy and immature, was put with the heavy old brood mares in the nursery pasture.

3

BY MARCH LIFE had changed a little for Kiko. For one thing, he was eleven years old and this seemed a vast step ahead, much more important than going from nine to ten. At first it had been disturbing to notice that he'd grown not much bigger. Eleven sounded like a tall age and Kiko was smaller than boys that age at school. He decided, however, that by next year he'd be bigger, and ceased to worry about it.

Another change was that there was a new child, his own size, living on the ranch. Unfortunately, the child was a girl; unfortunately, he learned that she was a whole year older than himself.

His father had told him, "There's some people from back East, friends of Mr. Richie's, going to live in the guest house awhile. Maybe they'll have some kids your age you could play with, unless they're stuck-up kind of people. The man writes books. Maybe he's going to write one about cowboys and horses, maybe that's why they're coming."

Kiko said, "I don't want any other kids bothering around. I got my burro." But just the same he was curious and when these people came he viewed their arrival from a safe distance.

"Only an ole girl," he thought. The girl's name was Amy Fairfield, and he watched her, a thin, pale child with long yellow braids, jump out of the car and hurry ahead of her parents up the garden path to the guest house door. She was, he decided, no one he need bother about.

But there came the morning when he could no longer ignore her. The two children stood together, waiting for the school bus.

Amy smiled at him and said in a small voice, "I like that donkey I see you riding sometimes."

"Donkey? Oh, that is my burro, Sancho." Then, realizing that she knew nothing about anything connected with life on the ranch, Kiko began to feel important, the way people do when they can pass on information. "My burro is very good. Maybe I will let you ride him sometime."

"Oh, I'd like that." The bus had come up the hill, passed the ranch on the way to the reservation, soon would return with the Indian children, then go on to pick up more children from ranches down in the valley. School was about twelve miles away.

Amy wanted to say more to this boy; soon he would be the only

13

familiar child among a number of strangers. She happened to say the exact right thing. "I hope you will show me around the ranch. I want to see all the horses and everything."

"When we get home from school I will show you many things," he promised.

To spend a green and gold afternoon in March looking at horses was a refreshing thing to do after Amy's first day in a new school. Not that she hadn't gotten along all right. She had, but she was naturally somewhat shy, and the day had been an ordeal.

She had had to sit in the middle of the bus and Kiko had not sat with her. The Indian children had crowded into the rear, and because of a stranger on the bus they had kept silent. She felt that they were staring at her and she looked steadily out of the window. Once in awhile she thought she heard a giggle and she wondered if they laughed at her because she was new.

One girl smiled at her shyly as they were getting off the bus in front of the school, but she didn't learn until later that this was Kiko's cousin, Anatasia.

That afternoon, Kiko and Amy wandered through the pastures and stood looking at the brood mares—bays and blacks and chestnuts and two grays, all beginning to shed their winter coats, ready to be groomed bright and shining by the season. The mares were ponderous now, with deep and thoughtful eyes. Kiko pointed out that very soon the new foals would come to the pasture.

"But look at that one, not nearly so big."

"This is Mia, I like her the best." Kiko petted the mare and she touched the faces of the children and ruffled their hair with her breath. "Even Mr. Richie used to like her the best."

14

Kiko had been giving Mia extra attentions ever since the day, nearly a year ago, when she had run off to the reservation. He had felt a deep sadness about her and the foal within her, and with a desire to do something for her he took her bits of good things to eat. Mia consumed offerings of left-over tortillas, apple cores and carrots, happily unaware that the future of herself and her unborn was not a happy thing.

Seeing her enjoy what he brought comforted Kiko but in no way solved what he knew to be a big and terrible problem. To give her pleasure in little ways was the only thing he could think of to do for Mia.

Amy said, "How soft her coat is. Why is she smaller than the others?"

"She will be only two years old when she foals. She is much too young. Perhaps she will die. Anyway, if she is very sick and doesn't snap right out of it and grow, probably they will shoot her. They will shoot the colt anyway."

The girl said nothing. She looked at him with an expression of such horror and unbelief in her blue eyes that he turned away.

"Oh, I know!" he said, and very nearly sobbed.

"But why?"

"Oh, because—" He took a deep breath. How could he explain what he himself could scarcely understand, about adults and the way they ran affairs? "Well, she is too young. And she ran to the reservation and there was a scrub stallion there. Mr. Richie was the maddest we ever seen him. The foal will not be very good. My father told me. Mr. Richie can't have any but the best to sell, and he couldn't even give it away because someone would tell that it came off his

15

ranch. Mr. Richie doesn't like half-breeds," he added sadly.

Amy's city experience helped her to understand part of this. "Like a big important store won't sell damaged goods?"

"I guess."

"But this is different. This is something alive."

"I know. And my father said that because a mare is too young to foal won't hurt her if she doesn't have a real bad time. He says that little heifers and fillies won't grow big afterwards if they don't get enough to eat, but when they're fed well, like here, it wouldn't stop them from growing."

"But what does it matter? Mr. Richie has so much money he can afford to feed her."

"I don't know. He wants to make everything pay. He doesn't like to spend his money. I thought he might shoot Mia last spring, to save feeding her this long." He turned and put his face into her dark mane. "Poor, poor Mia."

Amy stood looking at the young mare, trying to think about the unborn. She had never seen a new foal. She had seen young animals in the zoo, and she had seen puppies and kittens. A colt, she thought, would be the most beautiful and wonderful of all.

The words she said next astonished herself almost as much as they did Kiko. She hadn't planned on saying them.

She spoke firmly. "We won't let them."

Never had Kiko heard such words. Never had he felt such consternation. Unable to speak, he stared at her with eyes like a patient dog's.

"Why not?" she persisted.

"Why not?" he echoed, while his mind fumbled for a thousand

reasons. First there was "Authority" which had always terrified him. It terrified the Indians on the reservation, it terrified his father, it had terrified his grandparents. "We couldn't."

"Why couldn't we?"

"Because . . . . . "

4

THE NEXT MORNING while they waited for the bus Amy said, "I didn't sleep last night. I have it all planned."

"No," Kiko answered.

"We will have to be brave. Listen. We will watch. When the colt is born we will take it and hide it."

"Where?"

"You know every place."

"It needs its mother's milk."

"We'd feed it out of a bottle."

"Where'd we get the milk?"

18

"Steal it somewhere."

"We can't. It wouldn't work."

"Why not?"

"Because—"

Kiko was thankful that the bus came just then. It was only a reprieve, but at least he would have time to think while he sat all day in school.

When they climbed off the bus that afternoon he was able to take up the conversation where he had left it. "Because a tiny foal needs to be fed many times all day and all night. Colts aren't like calves. A colt has to be with its mother all the time. We have to be away at school all the time."

"Isn't there any grownup we could trust?"

"You are a fool," he said angrily.

"I think you are a coward," she told him.

Kiko considered this calmly. He had, of course, been disobedient about many things. Many times he had been punished.

But all this was a different matter; this could lead to big trouble, this amounted to strong warring against Mr. Richie, against everything overwhelmingly big and important. It would be a revolt against what had frightened him all his life.

"Come on," Amy insisted. "Otherwise, all by myself I'll have to do something."

Her bravado was born of ignorance, but this Kiko didn't know how to explain. He pondered about where a colt could be hidden. And, he thought, there would have to be a goat to provide milk. So they'd have to hide a goat, too, and where would that come from? They'd have to add to their crime by stealing a goat from somewhere. The

19

colt would not like to be without its mother and would be squealing and whinnying all the time. He tried to explain this. "And when it got born how would we get it away from Mia? I think it would be too heavy to carry. And Mia would follow us, even jump the fence, and whinny so loud all the men would come running to look and see what was wrong."

Amy could think of no immediate reply to this. They had been standing just where the school bus had left them; now she started walking toward home. Kiko, wordless, walked with her.

Amy was still trying to make plans. "There must be a way, there's got to be."

The road took them by the brood mares' pasture and Mia, wondering if Kiko might have something for her, came to the fence. He had saved her an apple core from lunch.

Amy petted her, looked into her brown eyes.

"Kiko, there *is* a way! I know now! Listen." She spoke decisively. "We'll take Mia and hide her *before* the colt is born. It's easy."

"Easy!" he answered scornfully.

"Oh," Amy cried, "I thought Indians were brave. I thought Mexicans had revolutions and killed bad people."

Kiko gritted his teeth. "Americanos are fools."

"Then *you* are a fool. After all, you are an American boy because you were born on this very ranch. Tell me, Kiko, do you love Mia? Would you really like to see them shoot her foal and maybe shoot her too?"

"All right," he said. "We'll steal the mare. You have looked at television. You know what they do to horse thieves."

"We *aren't* stealing her. We are hiding her to save her and her

20

baby. We won't tell anyone. Not even if they torture us." Amy seized Kiko's shoulders, she shook him. "Kiko, do you understand? We *have* to."

He nodded. "But do you know what a thousand dollars is? Any of these mares are worth more than that."

"But if Mr. Richie thinks he might kill her she can't be worth much. And he'll kill the colt for sure."

"That is different." He tried for words to tell her how all that mattered. Mr. Richie would be furious if the mare disappeared. A mare from his ranch stolen and sold, bearing an inferior colt . . . Kiko gave up on that line of thought. "There will be the sheriff."

"Let him come. I won't tell him a thing."

To himself Kiko thought, "It is me the sheriff will bother. Not a rich white girl with a mother and father."

But there was no way of explaining about this.

Kiko had a bad night. He tossed and turned and argued with himself. But he knew what he knew—the important thing was Mia, the saving of Mia and her foal was what mattered. It was a better thought Amy had had, about hiding Mia, since it would be too difficult to hide her colt alone. This way Mia would be safe from Mr. Richie who might decide to have her killed. All this would be better and easier, after all. Possibly it could be done.

Kiko bolstered himself, remembering that he had outwitted his elders before. He had been caught and whipped, but it had been worth it.

That was when Mr. Richie had had the federal trapper come to the ranch. The coyotes weren't bothering the calves, healthy range

21

cows are able to protect their young very well. But Mr. Richie wanted all the foxes, bobcats, and coyotes destroyed as he was afraid they might eat quail eggs or kill young quail. This line of reasoning was completely beyond Kiko's comprehension. Why was it good for Mr. Richie to shoot quail, but bad for hungry coyotes to eat them?

Kiko had happened to see a tortured coyote struggling in a steel trap. Next he had seen a dead mother racoon in a trap, but her babies had not been dead and were trying to find milk. After that, Kiko had learned to look for a stake pounded in the ground, to poke with a stick to spring the traps hidden under a covering of earth.

He had taught his cousins on the reservation to spring traps, too, for their dogs were being caught and killed by the trapper. Kiko had managed to save a number of lives before he was caught and whipped. Now, thinking about it, he decided that he hadn't minded the whipping very much.

Perhaps it would be that way about Mia. Whatever he and Amy could do to try and save the mare and colt would be good to do, no matter what was done to him later. There was the chance that the whole project might turn out very well, that nothing would go wrong, that nothing bad would happen to him or Amy or Mia or the colt.

Amy didn't seem worried, but that was because she didn't know about things. It was because she was only a girl. A girl, he thought, could not be braver than a boy. Already she was dominating the situation, being determined and direct, showing qualities that Kiko, in his secret self, admired very much. But she didn't seem to realize how many plans would have to be laid—that he, the man, would have to do the planning and the work. When he thought of this Kiko suddenly grew up very much.

In the morning he looked like the same little boy in his faded, torn blue jeans, but really he was much older than when he had gone to bed.

It was Saturday and Kiko was up even earlier than when he had to go to school. He ate half a can of beans for breakfast, went outdoors and caught his burro and leaped on his back. Sancho needed no bridle; it was Kiko's custom to use only a lead rope, tied about the burro's neck and brought down to a half-hitch around his nose. In this manner it was easy to guide Sancho in the direction Kiko wished to go and handy when he wished to stop, for Sancho could then start grazing without the bother of a bit in his mouth.

As he rode through the early shadows he was wondering how to rouse Amy without annoying adults, in case Amy was still in bed asleep. But when he went along the fence of the brood mare pasture he spotted Amy, very much awake, petting Mia. She saw him and ran to the fence, scrambled over it, and demanded to know where he was going.

"I am going to look at a certain place. Can you come too?"

"Yes."

He guided Sancho close to the wooden fence. "Climb up and then slide on behind me."

The children rode south and then started down into a canyon, following a stony winding trail. "Get off here," said Kiko after awhile. "It is easier to walk down the steep places."

When they reached the shaded canyon floor the trail was level and soft and Kiko got back on the burro. He stopped beside a boulder and Amy climbed on and they followed a winding trail.

Suddenly Sancho stopped, his long ears alert. Kiko pointed. In a clearing under big live oaks three does, startled, lifted their heads to stare, then went bounding off up a brushy hillside. Amy had never before seen wild deer. Halfway up the canyon side the deer stopped to look down at the children and their burro, then hurried off to disappear in the brush.

The girl from the city was shivering with excitement. The sudden sight of the deer seemed magical to her, they were like animals out of a fairy tale. The way they had bounded off was as if they wore springs in their sharp little hoofs.

Kiko said, "They will have fawns in summer. They hide them at first, but once I saw a very tiny one."

Amy thought about all the lives that must be in the hills and the canyons. Baby things and mothers and fathers. Families of rabbits and coyotes and foxes and deer—there was no aloneness anywhere. Each one was busy living its own important life as best it knew how.

"There are cattle in this canyon, too," Kiko said, "but they must be grazing up on the hills. At noon they come down to the spring to drink."

"Is this still Mr. Richie's ranch?"

"Oh yes, this and much more. But we are going off it, the other way. There is a place I am thinking about."

"For Mia?"

"For Mia and her colt."

"You think we really can?"

"We have to."

With the green grass under the live oaks the canyon seemed as friendly as a park. "But won't they find her anywhere around here?"

24

Amy asked anxiously.

"Not around here. A place I know. Lots further."

5

THEY STOPPED AT the spring to sip some water. It came through a pipe out of the canyon side, poured into a big trough, overflowed, went on in a small stream to disappear into the sandy creek bed.

Sancho drank from the trough. Every time he swallowed his ears twitched. He held a mouthful of water, stood dreamily for awhile, then drank some more. Finally he let the water dribble out of his mouth.

"When he washes his mouth out like that he's all through drinking," Kiko explained.

"This is a nice spring."

26

"They call it Black Horse Spring. There really was a wild black horse, a stallion, once. He stole all the mares and no one could catch him. A long time ago."

"That's like a story. Oh, I wish he were still here! We could give Mia to him and Mr. Richie couldn't catch her." Amy imagined the hoof beats in the canyon filled with horses. "Mares and colts and a beautiful black stallion. He was beautiful, wasn't he?"

"Guess so. Well, we better go on."

The canyon twisted more, narrowed, and, as if suddenly making up its mind, curved decisively to the east. The children went on in the other direction, came to a barbed wire fence. Kiko slid off and opened a gate. "Now we are not on Mr. Richie's ranch. It stretches the other way. Now we are on the reservation."

"The reservation! But the road goes past our houses, the way the school bus goes."

"Yes, but there is this Black Horse Mountain. It is all reservation. We go now the same way the road goes, only there is this mountain. The reservation is the mountain and all the land around it there. And the Indians' houses," he said, pointing west, "are over on that side. No one ever comes to this part, it is too brushy."

Kiko's geography confused Amy. But it didn't matter. You followed the canyon until it went to the left, and you went to the right, and here was the fence and the gate, and up there was the mountain, all covered with brush and huge boulders.

There was no noticeable trail now. This was stony, brushy land. Kiko was walking, leading Sancho, and Amy followed Sancho's wispy tail until, suddenly, it vanished. She hurried. Now there was a forest of tall brush on either side, the trail beneath her feet was only an

27

old scar. Once it had been open and well traveled; now, unused, the brush had hidden it. But still you could follow the way it had gone, if, in the first place, you happened to know that it was there.

Gradually the trail climbed. And then suddenly there was an opening, a ledge, a little island of grass in the midst of brush, and a broken-down pole corral.

Kiko smiled gleefully. "It has stayed better than I thought. We can fix it up, we'll bring some baling wire tomorrow. Now if the spring still runs it is okay."

He dropped Sancho's rope and Sancho immediately began cropping the grass. The grass was in the sunlight now and the shadows were shorter. Amy stared around her.

"See," Kiko said. "No one can come here from that side. The brush is too thick. Only this way can you come, and everybody has forgotten about it. Not even the deer hunters from the city know about it."

"But who built the fence?"

"The hermit. I never saw him. It was a long time ago, my father said. The man, I guess he was a little loco, he got tired of people, he said they were too mean. He had some goats and he lived here. A long time ago, before even I was born."

"What happened to him?"

"I don't know. He died or went away or something."

"Did he have a real house?"

"Over here. See?"

But there was nothing to see but one adobe wall no higher than a pasture fence. The rest was all a jumble of broken adobe.

"Now," said Kiko, "we'll see about the spring."

28

They found the water, seeping from under a boulder, water coming from some ancient underground lake deep in the mountain. It formed a pool from which a deer could drink, trickled on, was absorbed by earth. "This is the most important thing of all," Kiko said triumphantly.

Amy was delighted. "No one would ever think to look here because no one would guess about this. They will think Mia is stolen and far away."

Kiko frowned. "Everything isn't going to be so easy."

"But we can do it anyway."

"Tomorrow can you come? We will fix the fence good. Next month is April and then the foal will be born." He was thinking that it would have to be planned just right. Leave Mia as long as possible in the pasture but get her here in time so that she would feel at home before the foal came. There was a great deal to worry about.

Amy said, "I have to go back. My mother might get mad if she doesn't know where I am."

This also was a problem. "What will they think?" Kiko asked. "We'll have to be here a lot."

"I don't think they'll care if I tell them I'm going off riding Sancho with you. Anyway, if we had to, we could sneak away at odd hours, at night or early in the morning. But I believe it will be all right. My mother really wants me to enjoy it here."

"Tomorrow we can say we are going down the canyon to play by the spring. I go all the time. My father knows I am safe. We can ask to bring our lunch. Tonight I will get some baling wire from the barn, we'll wire the fence all up good. I don't think she'll try to jump over now."

29

He sighed. There seemed to be a wall of problems ahead of them, but maybe if they planned just a little at a time things would work out.

The next day, Sunday, they worked while Sancho had a good time grazing near. The night before, Kiko had taken coils of baling wire and hidden them, with a pair of wire cutters, at the beginning of the canyon trail. With haywire anything can be patched, repaired or rebuilt. No one would care that the wire was gone; it is a product of no particular value, and there is always more of it.

Kiko had hidden something else in the brush of the canyon's rim. He had stuffed two feed sacks full of hay. This surprised Amy. "Can't she eat grass?"

"How long do you think that the grass in one corral is going to last?" he asked scornfully as he fastened the sacks together with a piece of wire, then tossed them over Sancho's back. The burro looked burdened with the sacks hanging down, one on each side, but it was not a heavy load. "We can take turns riding," Kiko offered.

"If we meet anyone they will ask what we have and where we are going?"

"We won't meet anyone today. The cowboys don't have to work on Sundays. Anyway, we could tell them we are just playing with our pack burro. We'll have to keep bringing feed whenever we can and hiding it until she'll need it."

"For today, anyway, it is lucky we don't have to go to Sunday School. I used to at home, back in New York, but here it is too far."

"Well, the padre doesn't come to the reservation church, only some

Sundays. Too far away and not enough people. When he comes my father and I go. He hopes to make me grow up good."

Kiko grinned at the thought of himself all grown and good.

"I'll have the first turn," he announced when they reached the canyon floor, and he rode the burro.

Trudging along behind him, Amy had no protests to offer. She saw that this was quite right. Kiko was planning everything wisely and well, things she hadn't thought about. She began to admire him and look up to him and know that she had been wrong when she had considered him a little boy to be ordered about.

She realized this further when they went to work on the corral. She didn't have the slightest idea about how to do anything until Kiko showed her. She remembered friends she had known when she lived in the city. Not one of them would know how to find his way around this country, what to do with a burro, how to save Mia and her colt.

They sat by the pool of the spring to eat lunch—peanut butter and jelly sandwiches for Amy, tortillas wrapped around beans for Kiko, food which Amy eyed with interest. "My aunt stopped by with some tortillas last night," Kiko said. "My father can cook beans but he can't make tortillas."

"I never ate any. Are they pancakes?"

"Here," offered Kiko, surprised to think that someone in the world hadn't eaten tortillas. "Here," said Amy, and traded a peanut butter and jelly sandwich for a tortilla and beans, which she liked very much.

"I'm thirsty," she announced finally.

"Drink then," said Kiko, surprised again.

"Here?" she asked, eying the pool with its golden-brown floor, see-

31

ing small bugs moving in its depths. She remembered something about being taught that water was not always safe to drink. It had to flow fast and purify itself.

"Like a horse drinks," said Kiko, lying on his belly and putting his lips to the water. "A horse moves a little of the top of the water first to brush off anything scummy. Then he drinks like this."

"Like this," said Amy and lay face down, too, but her braids fell over her shoulders and into the water and Kiko laughed.

"Isn't there water like this back East?"

"Lots more," she told him. "Back there the canyon would have a big brook in it all the time."

"Wait till summer comes and the grass all turns brown and hardly any springs are left. I hope this will keep for Mia."

"And the colt."

"And the colt."

"What will it be like, I wonder?"

Kiko shrugged. "Wait and see. We better get back to work," he said. "I'd like to get all this fixed today. We'll have to break a lot of brush and pile it along the weak places, and wire it to the old poles. There's lots to do. And before it rains again we have to figure out a dry place to keep the hay."

This was something else Amy hadn't thought about. Kiko certainly seemed to know about everything.

6

Y OU AND THAT little Mexican boy are together so much, what do you do all the time?" Amy's mother asked with interest. The Fairfields were just finishing dinner and Amy was enjoying her favorite dessert, apple pie with ice cream on it.

She swallowed a big mouthful. "He's only half Mexican; he's half Indian, too. Oh, we play. We ride the burro and we play we are explorers, and sometimes we look for gold. It's fun. We go look at the mares, too, and think about the colts they'll have in a month or two. Let's see, this is nearly the end of March. Soon some of them ought to start foaling. I can hardly wait. And, oh, Kiko told me the

33

most wonderful thing! Years and years ago there used to be a wild black stallion that lived down in the canyon and up on the mountain. I just love to think about him."

"You *are* having fun!" her mother agreed.

Amy's father said, "Kiko's a good little kid. I've talked to Frank. He's done a good job raising him."

"Frank's name is really Francisco," Amy informed him. "That means Francis, but Mr. Richie likes to call him Frank. He thinks Francisco sounds too Mexican, I guess. Mr. Richie is odd. You know, when Kiko and I happen to run into him he always says hello to me, but he has a funny way of looking right through Kiko, as if he didn't see him. Kiko's name is Francisco, too, only Kiko is the nickname. Kiko knows all about the horses and cattle and everything. When they work the calves this spring he's going to let me go with him and look."

"Work the calves?"

"They round up all the cattle and put all the cows and calves in the corral. The cowboys rope the calves and they brand them and earmark them and vaccinate them for something, and burn off where their horns would grow. Kiko says they're real mean to little calves, but he's used to it. Only he thinks I won't like to look and maybe I won't. He says all these things have to be done but that the calves soon forget all about it and run and play the same as ever."

"I wouldn't like that part about ranch life," her mother said, "but I really do enjoy living out in the country this way. This is a very beautiful place. Sometime I want to learn to ride a horse."

"I know a girl at school who has her own horse. I wish I did. Daddy, do you think I could?"

"I don't know. See how this book goes, see how long we stay here. We'll see."

"We'll see" was a phrase grownups liked to use. Ordinarily it was a frustrating expression, but now Amy didn't mind. She found it entertaining to think that she and Kiko had a terrific secret from all the grownups in the world. If only they could guess! But they wouldn't believe it anyway.

The next day after school Kiko and Amy visited the brood mares again, stared at Mia. "I can truly see her with my eyes shut, we've looked at her so much," Amy said. "Shouldn't we take her soon now? Should we go in the middle of the night, or early in the morning, or when? How are we going to do it, anyway?"

"We'll see," Kiko said.

"Kiko, what do you suppose will happen? How bad will it be when they find Mia gone? What do you suppose they'll do?"

This was a subject Kiko didn't like to discuss. It frightened him very much. "It will be bad," he answered. "I told you before."

"I wish we knew exactly what to expect."

"The sheriff will come. Everyone will ask questions. Everyone will be going around looking for Mia. And Mr. Richie, he'll be madder than he's ever been. I hope he won't fire my father. He scares me—"

"But how can they guess about us? And how can they find her there where we'll hide her? Oh, I wish everything would hurry up! I want to get the scary part over as soon as possible."

Kiko didn't reply. He was studying Mia intently.

Kiko had a quiet patience that exasperated Amy.

By April the wild lilac was thick on the hills, waves of blue and purple and foamy white, moving with the wind. All the air was honey-sweet. Flowers were in the grass—little yellow violets, white popcorn flowers, baby blue-eyes, wild primroses, many more; flowers Amy had not known about. Birds sang all the time. She wakened every morning to their wild sweet songs.

Mia was heavy now, and quiet. Her rich bay coat was shining, her black mane glistened in the sunshine, her eyes looked wise and deep. The star on her forehead seemed bigger, whiter. Fearful of arousing suspicion, the children appeared to pay no particular attention to her. They went into the brood mare pasture and looked at all the mares, petted several, didn't touch Mia, but Kiko observed her with knowing eyes.

Finally they agreed to choose a starlit night when the waning moon rose late. It should be midweek so that both children would be in school the following day, something that might help avert suspicion. This was hard to bear, as they would have preferred to spend a long day with Mia in her new home.

There came a morning when, as they waited for the school bus, Kiko seemed to be deep in thoughts of his own. He paid not the slightest attention to anything Amy said. "Whatever is wrong with you?" she asked him, exasperated. But he didn't hear that, either.

The bus came down the road from the reservation and as they started to get on Kiko appeared to have made up his mind. He turned to Amy swiftly. "Tonight," he whispered. "I have decided."

Amy said nothing and sank limply into her seat. For some time now they had been moving toward this moment. Now that it was upon them she wished almost to postpone it. It was really and truly about to happen. Mia would disappear, the sheriff would come.

Her bravado began to crumple. What if everything went wrong, what if the law put a stern hand on the shoulders of herself and Kiko? This was not impossible. What would her parents think as they dragged her off to jail? What would she feel if her father looked at her out of hard eyes, or, worse, looked right through her as Mr. Richie looked at Kiko? Could she bear it?

Anyway, it was settled now. No backing out. In her heart she didn't want to back out, not truly. She shut her eyes and pictured Mia. Then she tried to see the colt, warm and alive by Mia's side. The colt that wasn't going to be allowed to live unless Mia were hidden on the mountainside. From its soft dark place the unborn demanded love and care.

Amy learned nothing whatsoever at school that day.

That night Amy went to bed at her usual time. She lay awake and listened. It seemed that never had it taken so long for her parents to go to bed. She had to wait a long while to be sure they were asleep, then make herself wait longer yet. Count slowly to one hundred. Count to two hundred. Say all her prayers again. (This she felt to be a very good idea. She and Kiko and Mia needed all possible help.)

Amy thought she made a great deal of noise as she got out of bed, dressed in the dark. She carried her shoes and stepped softly, held her breath, shivered with nervousness until she thought her teeth would rattle, would sound like loud castenets. There were no doors to open. Earlier she had unlatched the window screen, gone to bed with the window open. She had only to climb out and stand on the grass.

Now she was glad there were no ranch dogs.

Because she had not come from a lighted room, her eyes were

willing to see in the night. She stood practising seeing, looking at dark trees and buildings, at a dim road. She breathed the sweet air, listened to all the little rustling sounds of night. She wanted to run but she was afraid she might fall over something, make a sound.

She hoped Kiko would be with Mia in the pasture. Whoever got there first would wait for the other, and Amy felt herself too excited to bear being able to wait.

Kiko was there, standing quietly, petting Mia. Already he had the lead rope on her. Some of the mares were lying down, some stood sleepily, some were grazing. They were accustomed to the children and didn't register surprise that they were there at this hour.

They led Mia across the grass, through the gate. No mare whinnied and Kiko sighed with relief. If this were summer and dusty, there would be a greater worry about leaving tracks. Even so, it would be better if this were a night of rain to erase all marks, but the time of rain was too unpredictable and the time for the foal was soon.

They walked on no trail. With the morning dew grass would re-cover soon from having been trod upon. Getting down into the canyon was slow going as they stayed off the trail and wound through the brush where they hoped they were leaving no clear sign. On the canyon floor was Sancho, standing where Kiko had tied him. Mia whinnied softly, glad to see him, and Sancho started to bray. Kiko grabbed him by the nose. Amy giggled nervously.

"So far, *bueno*," Kiko said softly.

Amy looked at the big bright stars above the canyon rim. They must have shone on all kinds of secret happenings, but this, she thought, was surely one of the very best.

"I'll walk ahead with Mia," Kiko told Amy. "You ride Sancho right behind so if tracks show they'll be burro tracks. I'll stay off the trail as much as I can."

Something white showed by the canyon spring and for the first time Amy felt frightened, but it was the white faces of resting cattle turned inquiringly toward them. "Are you scared?" she asked Kiko, still speaking in a half-whisper.

"Naw! What of?" But Amy thought he was slightly scared. After all, he was only eleven years old.

The cattle seemed somewhat alarmed at the intrusion of mare, burro and children, and, as they started getting to their feet, Kiko had an idea.

"Stand still with Sancho," he ordered. "I'm going to circle around with Mia and get ahead of them. They're scared now and ready to go, so when I have time to get a little ahead, you and Sancho kind of shoo them. Don't let them break back up the canyon. Head them down the canyon behind Mia. They'll cover up her tracks real good."

Like shadows, Kiko and Mia vanished toward the canyon side. Amy tried to count the shapes of the cattle. There were, she decided, only about eight or nine of them. They were uneasy now, ready to go, as Kiko had said.

"Shoo!" she called softly, feeling strangely timid, moving Sancho toward them. "Shoo, get going!"

They did, and rather swiftly. She heard the soft thud of their cloven hoofs. Then, sensing, or seeing, Mia ahead, they slowed, no doubt feeling that it was strange to be driven anywhere at this hour, but accepting it as part of the odd ways of humans and horses.

Sancho pattered along eagerly, not wanting to lose track of Mia, paying attention to the cows he was driving. As they proceeded, two

39

cows managed to lose themselves in the brush, but most of them traveled along at a cautious distance behind Mia. This laying of cow tracks on top of Mia's tracks was an unexpected bit of good luck.

Amy and Kiko had already timed the trip. It had taken not quite an hour to reach the corral, but now it seemed to be taking twice that long. As they turned off toward their mountain they parted company with the cattle. The cows went wandering in the other direction to find a place to settle down for the rest of the night. Amy felt like telling them, "Thank you very much."

The hidden brushy trail up the mountain was in a forest of wild lilac, but in the darkness Kiko did not take one step astray.

They offered Mia a drink at the spring pool; she looked down on reflected stars, touched the water gently, but was not thirsty enough to drink. Some days before, Kiko had removed a bucket from the ranch and now he had it full of water in the corral. It would be wise for Mia to drink now, saving it for some future hour, but she wouldn't.

Kiko led her through the gateway, turned her free, wired the bars firmly. She walked around, dropped her head, began to graze. The children would have liked to watch longer to make sure she would stay quietly, but they felt they should hurry in case, somehow, someone might notice that they were not in their beds.

As they started to leave, Mia flung up her head and whinnied, her white star very clear in the night.

"I don't know—" muttered Kiko, and they went on.

The whinnies became wilder, louder. They heard Mia's galloping hoofs. "She'll never stay," Amy lamented. "Now what?"

"I planned for this," said Kiko calmly. "I didn't really want to do it, though." They turned back. He tied the lead rope he had used on Mia to the rope Sancho wore; it made a long piece. He tethered Sancho to a bush outside the corral where there was grass. "Now," he said, "they can keep each other company. Sancho will have to stay here until the colt comes, to keep Mia from being lonesome."

"Listen!" Amy exclaimed, her spine shivering.

"Only coyotes," Kiko assured her.

"What about coyotes? What about if there's a mountain lion? Couldn't something happen to Mia and her colt?"

"Maybe. But I think no. Mr. Richie is worse."

Amy saw what he meant. "It's people we have to be afraid of, isn't it?"

"It's people that want to kill the colt and maybe Mia, too. I think she will be safe in these hills."

Amy began to feel better—and braver. "Oh, Kiko, we've done it! We've got Mia safe, and her colt will live, and everything's going to be all right!"

"Yes," said Kiko. "I guess so."

"Everything will be wonderful," she exulted.

"I guess so," he repeated as they started on the dark walk home. But already he was beginning to worry about many things.

7

Almost to their surprise, the next day started uneventfully. The children were not wakened at dawn by some authoritative person shaking them, demanding to know what they had done with Mia. Only in Amy's dreams had this happened. They rose, ate, got ready for school as usual; the only thing different was that they were extra-sleepy this morning.

They yawned as they waited for the school bus. Kiko said, "I don't think anyone's even noticed yet that she's gone."

Certainly everything seemed calm. No sheriff's car came racing up the road, no groups of men were gathered around talking.

Someone always looked at the brood mares, twice a day at least, but someone could glance across the pasture, see that everything appeared all right, and not observe that one was gone.

When they reached the ranch after school the same peaceful state seemed to exist. This gave them a strange feeling. They had fully expected the sheriff to meet them as soon as the bus stopped. Nothing was happening—but something was going to happen. The uncertain quiet made them extremely uneasy.

"Maybe they know and they're just waiting to trap us." Kiko spoke in a whisper.

"It does seem too good. But I think it's all right. Let's hurry and see how Mia and Sancho are."

Amy didn't take time to eat an after-school snack. She pulled on her jeans and went sailing out the door. "Where are you off to in such a hurry?" her mother called.

"Oh, we left Sancho down the canyon. We want to go find him."

Kiko was halfway to the canyon floor before she caught up with him. He warned, "We better stay off trails as much as we can. The less tracks we leave the better."

They ran whenever the came to a good place for running; they didn't stop for a drink at Black Horse Spring.

Kiko observed with satisfaction that the grass by the wire gate looked untrampled. They crawled under the fence a short distance from the gate. "Someone might notice if the trail by the gate looks worn," he explained.

They hurried up the trail between the heavy lilac blossoms. They reached the clearing and Mia looked up and nickered at them. Sancho, safely tied, stared and twitched one long ear. The children collapsed on the grass to rest and enjoy the fact that here all was well.

As soon as it was easy to breathe again, Kiko took Sancho for a drink. He untied the ropes he had tied together for Sancho, used one to lead Mia to water while Amy held the burro. When Mia was back in the corral he refilled her water bucket, then retied the two ropes and tethered Sancho in fresh grass. He gazed at Mia thoughtfully. "Not for a couple of days, I think."

"Only a couple of days," Amy thought, and wondered fearfully about what might happen in this short time before Mia foaled. Surely the ranch hands must have missed her by now. If they had not they soon would.

If the men rode and looked everywhere, they might easily find her, this place might not be as safe as she and Kiko planned that it should be.

"It isn't so much for myself that I'm frightened," Amy told Kiko anxiously. "But if they should find Mia now and take her back, we just couldn't hide her again. I don't know what we'd do. It would be too awful!"

"They'd do plenty to us, too," Kiko said darkly.

"Well," said Amy, "it's no use considering all that now. She's here. And everything can turn out all right. It's just that I get extra scared sometimes, thinking of what could happen. We ought to be thinking about the colt, that's what's important."

"That's better than thinking about Mr. Richie. I like to think about that colt," Kiko said, cheering up.

"Wouldn't it be wonderful if she has it Saturday? Then we'd have all that day with it, and Sunday too."

"Well," said Kiko, "you never can tell."

44

"Should we give her a little hay?"

"She has plenty of grass; we better save the hay until she needs it. After the foal comes we can take Sancho home and haul down more hay."

The hay was safe, tucked where boulders had formed almost a natural cave where it would keep dry in the April rains. There were many such places on the mountain where, Amy thought, foxes and coyotes could raise their babies. For Mia and Sancho there was no shelter in case it rained. But Kiko said that it didn't matter, they were used to being in the open, even in snow.

Amy looked around her. The late sun was extra golden on the green grass, wild sweet peas climbed the chaparral and decorated sagebrush and greasewood with deep rose colors.

"Listen!" Kiko said suddenly, and they heard a canyon wren dropping notes one by one down the scale.

"You only hear them in real wild places. At home in the pastures there are meadow larks but they don't come here. And canyon wrens don't go there."

"A wild place is a safe place for Mia," Amy thought. She looked south, toward dim mountain ranges, thought of all the good places safe from people. She stood up and started picking wild sweet peas, planning to twine them in Mia's mane, but Kiko said, "We better hurry home now."

To their astonishment, the next morning was again peaceful. Amy downed her apprehension and giggled as she and Kiko waited for the bus. "They don't even know that she is gone."

"They'll find out pretty soon," said Kiko.

When they got off the bus that afternoon Kiko's father met them, riding one of the quarter horses. "I just been up to the reservation," he told them. "Mia's got out, or got stolen, maybe last night. I can't find no tracks. You better get the burro, Kiko, and ride around and look." Amy thought that Kiko trembled visibly, but his father didn't seem to notice.

"I'll go get Sancho. He's down the canyon."

"I'll go too," Amy said.

"Why would she get out?" Kiko asked his father, suddenly becoming crafty.

"I don't know. It's funny."

"Was she going to have a colt?" Amy inquired innocently. "Maybe she ran away to hide and have it."

"I can't figure it. I'll have to phone Mr. Richie now and see what he says to do."

"Has she been gone long?" Amy wanted to know. "When did you see her last?"

"I guess she was here all right yesterday. No one noticed she was gone until this afternoon. But she must have gone in the night. There's no tracks, though. It beats me."

"Come on, Kiko," Amy said. "Let's look for her."

They were joyful as they descended into the canyon. From time to time Amy called, "Mia, Mia," and sounded so convincing that she made Kiko laugh.

Two of the ranch hands came riding along. "You kids didn't see a loose mare?" one of them asked.

"We're looking for her now," Kiko answered. "My father told us about her."

46

"We didn't see a sign of her down that way." And the men rode on.

"I'll be glad when we can bring Sancho back," Kiko said uneasily. "Someone might start to wonder."

"I don't think they will. No one pays much attention to Sancho and us. We're just off playing somewhere; we're just kids."

Again all was well with Mia and Sancho. "We don't have to hurry back because they think we're out looking for the mare," Kiko said. "And now we should walk her a little, it would do her some good. Anyway, let her eat awhile on this grass outside and save the corral grass."

They led Mia around the clearing, letting her graze. The last thing, when she was thirsty, they took her to drink. "Look," said Kiko, entranced. "There's something I bet you never saw before. The cold water makes it do it when the mare drinks."

"What?" asked Amy. And then she saw, near the mare's flank, the motion of the unborn foal. It was a fluttering liveliness, as if a baby bird were trying its wings.

Kiko grinned. "He wants out!"

Mia sighed and shifted her feet.

"I wonder what she thinks it is, all that kicking in there. Oh, I wonder what it looks like. Kiko, I can hardly wait!"

"We'll find out one of these days pretty soon."

When they got home there was the sheriff's car, pulled up by the fence of the mares' pasture. "Good-by," said Kiko and started for his house.

"Hey!" an authoritative voice called. "You kids come here a minute."

"Don't look so scared," Amy whispered. "We don't know any-

47

thing, they won't hurt us." But she felt terror. Here it was, just as they'd pictured it, sheriff and all. Several sheriff's men, in fact. Even as she reassured Kiko she felt her own knees shaking, for there was Mr. Richie, who had rushed out from town, staring at them exactly as if he read their thoughts. Kiko's father stood near, and several of the ranch hands were talking with one another.

"The whole thing is ridiculous," Mr. Richie was saying. "That mare's caused me nothing but trouble. Where can she be, anyway?"

The brisk young sheriff's deputy had no desire to frighten children. "We just wonder, did either of you kids hear anything in the night? Or have you seen any strangers around lately? Where have you been just now?"

Amy spoke up. "We were looking for the mare. Kiko's father told us to. We didn't find her, though. No, we haven't seen anyone around lately, but we're in school most of the time. I didn't hear anything in the night, did you, Kiko?"

Kiko shook his head.

It was plain that no one could understand how Mia could have vanished without a trace.

"She's got to be located, and soon," Mr. Richie said. "I'm not going to leave a stone unturned."

For the men it was futile to ride around looking for a mare that had disappeared so mysteriously, leaving not the slightest clue as to what had happened. The country was too vast for such a search and, anyway, Mia wasn't likely to be hiding behind some clump of brush. There had to be some logical place to look. So far, the only likely place that anyone could think of was the Indian reservation, for Mia had gone there once before. Three men began a search of the reservation. They scoured it thoroughly, the Indians offering no help at all. After that, they rode around aimlessly. What was the use? If you can't track a strayed animal, if you have no idea in which direction it might have gone, it would be only by the greatest stroke of luck that you'd come across it. Because that stroke of luck might happen, Mr. Richie insisted that a few of the men keep riding and searching. But even he realized that this was a waste of time.

During the next few days the children, likely to meet men on horses at any time, were cautious and nervous as they neared the place where they must leave the canyon to creep under the fence and hurry to disappear in the brushy trail. Kiko saw by the tracks that someone had ridden to the wire gate. Obviously, whoever it had been had seen no tracks beyond the gate, had concluded that no one had used it for a long time, that probably the mare wouldn't be in this area anyway. So far as the children knew, this was as close as any searcher had got to Mia.

Kiko knew of a certain spot, up the mountain from the corral, that made a perfect look-out. He could creep out on an overhanging boulder, lie flat on his belly, and have a good view of the lower part of the canyon and the wire gate. Every time they visited Mia he hurried there to watch and to make sure that they hadn't been followed.

One afternoon he reported to Amy, "My father told me that the men think now that someone led Mia out at night and was careful not to leave tracks. They walked her to where they must have loaded her into a truck or trailer. Mr. Richie is going to have auctions watched all over everywhere in case she shows up."

49

"It's odd," said Amy. "He doesn't really love Mia, but he has to have her back."

"My father says Mr. Richie can't have mares disappearing—especially Mia who'll have a scrub foal."

Fortunately for Kiko and Amy, none of the grown people seemed to remember what it had been like to be a child. No one really considered the children. No one realized that the children had a direct and simple view of things, that to them the life of a foal was of value. No one thought to look at the situation through a child's eyes or he would have discovered what a reasonable and natural thing it was to remove the mare and her unborn from danger. The mystery that had seemed so complicated was simple, so simple that no one could solve it.

If, for a moment, anyone did happen to have a fleeting suspicion that the children knew more about Mia's disappearance than they were telling, the thought was soon abandoned. Kiko didn't appear to be a very resolute child. Of course last year he had been a naughty little boy and had sprung a lot of coyote traps, but that had no bearing on the present situation. A boy like Kiko and a little girl fresh from the city couldn't possibly be horse thieves.

Not knowing what the adults' line of reasoning might be, the children continued to be furtive and watchful. Each day after school the canyon swallowed them. They approached the corral with their hearts thumping loudly, excited and hopeful. Maybe this day there would be the foal.

But Mia continued to wait, and she seemed even more dreamy and thoughtful and slow to move. Her eyes were deep brown liquid into which the children stared as if trying to read her intentions.

"It will be a horse colt," Kiko decided. "They wait longer than a filly, and get bigger, I think."

Neither child happened to consider that if the foaling were difficult Mia would be in real trouble. In this secret, remote place how would she get help? Not even Kiko seemed to realize that, without meaning to, they had placed Mia's life in danger. If the thought had occurred to him he would have been frightened, but he would have reasoned further and told himself that it had to be this way.

The range cows seldom had trouble producing their little white-faced calves; most of the mares foaled with no interference from any-one. The business of birth had been going on for a long time before human beings ever knew enough to worry about it. Trouble might be expected for Mia because she was too young and too small, but she was healthy, she had exercise, and she was not overfed. Nature had made a mistake by letting so young a mare get with foal in the first place. Now nature would have to be the only midwife.

These visits to Mia were frustrating for Amy because she dared not stay away from home too long. Her parents were firm about enforc-ing the rule that she must be on time for dinner. Nearly two hours of every afternoon were spent hurrying along on foot, either on the way to Mia or on the way home to dinner, which was at six-thirty.

She realized that once the colt was born it was going to be even more frustrating. How could she turn her back on the little new being to hurry home, eat dinner, do her homework, take a bath and go to bed? At least, Amy told herself, if she could live through part of April, all of May, and a week of June, it would be summer vacation and surely then there would be long hours to spend with Mia and the colt. She felt a fierce and protective love for this foal, this un-

51

known one unwanted by any except herself, Kiko, and Mia.

Kiko was lucky. There were no regular hours at his house. Sometimes his cowboy father didn't get home until dark; a cow or calf to be doctored, a fence to be repaired—anything could happen to keep Frank working late.

Very often Amy hurried home alone while Kiko stayed to take Mia walking around the clearing, a form of exercise which he believed might hasten the birth of the colt.

8

IT HAPPENED ON a Friday afternoon. First the children saw the long
ears of Sancho, stiff with attention, standing straight up. He was
staring into the corral, his nostrils flared with excitement. Immediately the children heard Mia speak, nickering in a very deep soft
voice, as a mare speaks only to her new-born.

There lay the colt, shining wet and shivering, struggling to do
something worthwhile with all his long legs. Mia was nosing him,
licking him, encouraging him to take a firm hold of life.

"I think it has just happened," Kiko whispered. "He's all wet and
he hasn't stood up."

Amy burst into tears. "Mia's all right, isn't she? And the colt's going to live?"

Without taking his attention from the colt Kiko whispered, "Of course they're all right. Why do you cry?"

Amy sobbed, "I am so happy," and stared at the miracle on the grass. "I want to go touch it."

"Wait," advised Kiko. "From here we will watch awhile. Don't get Mia too excited."

The colt decided that his front legs might be of use, braced them before him, pushed with his folded back legs, rose. But the shaking legs weren't ready, the colt pitched forward and went down. Mia nickered anxiously and Amy cried, "Oh!"

"Only the first try," Kiko explained wisely. "They never make it the first time."

"Isn't anything wrong?"

"Nothing is wrong."

"Look, Kiko, he is not the color of Mia."

"He is going to be a black horse."

"He flops like a fish out of water. Are you sure he's all right?"

"Watch."

The colt uttered a funny whickering sound which made Amy laugh and made Mia speak to him earnestly. "How does she know what to do?" Amy asked.

"She knows."

Floundering about in his attempts to stand warmed the colt, made the blood circulate as his little heart pumped busily. He got on his feet again and staggered two steps before he fell and landed on his side. It didn't take so long to sort out his legs this time, and he was up, teetering so dangerously that, unable to restrain themselves, the children crawled under the fence to help him. Mia didn't mind in the least. These two she trusted.

Carefully Kiko guided his wavering steps. "Hold still, Mia. Whoa." They got the colt's nose to the udder, they saw his pink gums as his lips parted; in a minute he was tugging strongly and immediately the milk gave him strength. Mia lifted one back leg, squealed because her udder felt tight and hurt a little, but she did not move away. She turned her head to touch the small rump with her nose.

Amy stopped holding her breath. "He's so scrawny."

"He'll fill out."

"Are they always so little and skinny?"

"Some are. He'll be all right."

"His eyes are like little buttons, and his mane's all kinky. And he's wagging his tail!"

Kiko snorted. "You speak like he's a dog. Sometimes they swish their tails when they nurse."

"His toes curl up," noticed Amy, dismayed. "I mean the end of his hoofs—look—like Turkish shoes. He walks on his heels."

"That will be all right too."

"Do they always?"

"Not all of them. He may be weaker than some, but not very. That'll be all right in a couple of days. Wait and see."

Amy sighed. "I think he is perfectly beautiful."

The colt felt so good as he finished drinking that he tried a slight caper. Looking like a rocking-horse, he cantered three slow steps and didn't fall down. Then he put down his nose, folded his legs correctly. and settled for his first nap. Mia had to keep touching him, feeling him all over, and then she too lay down. She was tired.

The children lay on their bellies close to the colt, touching him gently with their fingers. Kiko pointed out that the cups of his hoofs were filled with a soft gristle-like substance. "Why?" asked Amy.

"My father says to keep the mare from getting hurt while it's being born. This drops out pretty soon."

The colt went sound asleep, breathing very fast, and he had his first little dream and nickered while he slept.

Colts and calves and lambs, baby goats, piglets and others have an advantage over puppies, kittens and human babies. They are born wide awake, with open eyes, ready, almost at once, to move around and view the world.

The colt's first nap was brief. Soon he was up. He did much better this time. Mia got to her feet and he tasted milk again, then walked about, though Mia kept so near that the two seemed glued together.

He was so small that he could walk right under her belly, and he did. His little neck curved, his forehead had the wise bulge that new foals wear. He wobbled as he walked, his hoofs pointed skyward, and his hind legs had a rabbity look. As he dried, the children could see that he was the color of a mouse.

"He'll be black," Kiko foretold. "Black horses usually are this mouse gray when they are born. And gray horses lots of times are born black."

Mia was very slick and shining now, with red-gold tints in her coat. Kiko's eyes kept exploring the lines of mare and colt, comparing. The colt had slanting shoulder bones, a good chest; Kiko noted the legs and the long pasterns, the solid miniature hoofs.

56

Amy observed the shining little eyes, the short mane and tail, all frizzly and black and soft. The small folded nostrils enchanted her; she kissed the colt's nose, admired his pointed ears.

Mr. Richie would have looked at the skimpy little thing and called for a gun. Mr. Richie would have been remembering the appearance of the colt's sire, he would not have seen what the children saw.

Kiko said, "He will be a fine big horse some day."

Amy answered thoughtfully, "He is so dear and so sweet now. I hope he won't change for a long time."

"He will change in three days. He will fill out and be even prettier. You wait."

"There is Saturday and Sunday," Amy exulted. "But how can we bear to go home now?"

"After dark I will bring a blanket and come back," Kiko decided. "After I am sure my father is asleep."

"I wish I could."

"You better not. But I will come and see that they are all right tonight. Some animal might bother, but I think not."

"We won't have to leave Sancho here any more."

"No, and he'll wish he could stay here. He likes the colt. My father says that old jackasses will kill colts, but that's different. Sancho is a gelding, and he's seen lots of colts, and he and Mia like each other. And the colt won't be afraid of him because even Mia doesn't know what a burro can do. A burro stallion can even kill a horse stallion bigger than him, my father told me. But if Mia and none of them knows, they will all like each other. You have to go home now. We don't want them to wonder about us too much. Soon I will come on Sancho, and then I will come back here. But first we must water the mare. I think we'll not take her to the spring, we'll carry the bucket."

Mia was thirsty. It took four buckets before she was satisfied. Amy lingered as long as she dared, thinking what a beautiful place this was to be born in, with birds singing all around, and the air good with the smell of grass and flowers.

She ran as much as she could on the way home. She met no living things but birds and a fast-hopping brush rabbit, and she thought that the colt would soon be noticing rabbits and wondering about them and watching the deer come to drink at the pool. She and Kiko had observed the neat little tracks of the deer that had been to the spring, and she thought how lucky Kiko was to be with the colt all night and perhaps see the deer come in the morning.

9

IT TOOK AMY a long while to go to sleep that night. She kept wishing she were Kiko, sleeping right there in the corral.

Kiko had a good night. The very beginning of it wasn't so good, though, when, shortly after Amy left, he said good-by to the colt, assured him he'd be back as soon as he could, and started home on Sancho. Sancho hadn't been home since the night he'd been tethered outside the corral to keep Mia company. Now he was as excited as the children about the colt and he didn't want to leave it. Several times, hoping that Kiko wouldn't notice, he tried sneaking off the trail, planning to circle and turn back. Kiko was well aware of his plan and wouldn't let him carry it out. Sancho sighed drearily and plodded so slowly that Kiko swatted him with his rope end and kicked his sides with his heels. Kiko would have made better time if he had left Sancho there and walked.

It seemed to take his father an extra-long while to cook and eat supper that night. Kiko wasn't hungry, but he ate swiftly to get it over with. His father served himself more beans, enjoyed them, finally poured coffee and rolled a brown cigarette.

"How's school going?" he asked.

"All right. I'm glad tomorrow's Saturday, though. Maybe I'll ride out and look for Mia some more."

"That's a good thing to do, though you won't find her I think. Whoever took her, took her far away. Wonder if she's foaled by now?"

"It would be about time now, wouldn't it, Papa?"

"I guess it would. A funny thing, the whole business. I never seen Mr. Richie so mad. First he was mad when the mare got with the little stallion, now he's mad and upset because someone's got her."

"Do you suppose he'll ever find her?"

"Hard to say. I guess he'll find out something one of these days. Unless he gives up. I don't think he'll give up."

These words alarmed Kiko. His father was usually right, and if he thought that Mr. Richie would find Mia this was indeed a bad sign. For a short time Kiko had almost allowed himself to think that Mia was safe in her corral on the mountain. He sighed unhappily.

"What's the matter, boy? You tired?"

"Guess I am. I better go to bed so's I can get up early. There's a canyon over by the big canyon I want to look into."

"Everybody's looked everywhere," Frank said, "and never even saw a track."

"I know. But it's fun to do."

"Where you been keeping the burro lately? I haven't seen him in the corral."

"I been staking him out to graze. Saves hay."

Kiko yawned and so did Frank. "Maybe I'll turn in pretty soon myself."

"Guess we got spring fever," Kiko observed, and went to bed.

It seemed to take a long time before he heard his father snoring with encouraging steadiness. Then, carrying a blanket, Kiko crept outside.

There was no slowness about the trip back to Mia and the colt. Sancho wanted to start off loping, but Kiko made him walk so that no one would hear the sound of hurrying hoofs. Once down on the canyon floor he let Sancho go at his own speed and the burro loped steadily along the dark trail. The stars swung in the sky with the motion of Sancho's going. Kiko had never seen such pretty stars before.

He was careful, after he got past Black Horse Spring, to avoid leaving tracks on the main trail. He made the impatient burro wind through the brush, which made it slower going and exasperated them both.

In spite of this, they reached the corral more quickly than ever before. Mia heard them and Kiko could see her white star as her head shot up. He heard her alarmed snort.

"Mia, it's me!"

She quieted, put her head down to her sleeping colt. The colt wakened at once, scrambled up, and tried to see what was going on.

Sancho wouldn't think of going away now, but Kiko tethered him anyway. Otherwise, Sancho might try to get into the corral.

Mia spoke in a low voice to her colt. Kiko heard it nursing. He crept under the fence, stood petting Mia, and when the colt lay down he wrapped himself in his blanket and lay down near, so near that he could reach out his hand and touch a soft small rump.

The colt spent his first night on earth well guarded.

Kiko woke from time to time. A coyote called, putting a questioning sound into its voice. Another answered. Soon the sounds were as if a great number, up on the mountain, were chanting and singing a weird sort of music, punctuated by yappings. Kiko liked to see coyotes, but now their wild voices made him uncomfortable, they sounded so violent. Rabbits, foolishly unconcerned, hopped about in the corral. Kiko heard their thumping paws.

Later, Kiko heard the bark of a fox. By then Mia herself was lying down, but she stood up and Kiko could see the star on her forehead as she reached down to touch her foal. Night birds made quick twittering sounds, an owl spoke from some dark tree, and once Kiko saw a soundless stretch of wings between him and a star. There were continual rustlings in the brush.

Something crashed, sounding so big that Kiko trembled and sat straight up, worrying about a mountain lion. But it must have been only deer because Sancho and Mia were undisturbed. He saw Mia's white spot raised high as she sniffed the air to make sure that there was no danger. The colt slept on. Kiko could hear its quick, earnest little breaths. He reminded himself of what his father had told him so often, that wild animals didn't do half the damage they were accused of. It wasn't likely that any creature was prowling around looking for a colt to eat.

The night, he realized, was a safe time. In the night Mr. Richie wouldn't find the mare and colt. Daytime, when people wandered around, was far more dangerous. Night was a soft refuge for Mia and her colt. Feeling reassured, Kiko dropped off to sleep.

Later, coldness wakened him and he breathed in a stronger, sweeter smell from the brushy hills. It was the cool smell of morning. There came more small sounds now, and Kiko imagined that the night animals were going home to bed. The day shift was about to start; day animals were yawning, awakening. Hop toads moved toward their burrows. The stars were still bright and one that Kiko knew would still shine when the sky became pale with light.

Soon the colt would see his first daybreak. "Oh, I hope you will see many mornings, my little one," Kiko whispered to him. He caressed the colt, petted good-by to Mia, and crawled under the fence.

Again Sancho moved slowly and Kiko rode silently almost into a small herd of deer before, surprised, they bounded off, then turned to stare at him.

It was still not quite light when he reached home and went stealthily to bed. He didn't get up until he heard his father go off to work. Then he ate some beans and hurried to the feed barn, hoping that no one was there. He was in luck. No one was.

Having dreamed of the colt all night, Amy wakened early. She could scarcely wait to go to the corral. She made herself stay in bed until she heard her father get up and start making coffee, then dressed and hurried to the kitchen.

"You're up early," her father said, surprised. "It's Saturday. You could be asleep."

"I know. But Kiko wants to ride around on the burro and look for that mare. And I told him I was sure that you and Mother wouldn't care if I go too. So he said I could. May I make some peanut butter and jelly sandwiches to take?"

"You had better eat some cereal first. Else you'll be hungry before lunchtime. Your mother is still asleep, but I don't think she'll mind if you go. Just don't be too late getting home, will you?"

"I'll eat as soon as I get these sandwiches made. Oh, Daddy, it's so much fun living here. I wish we could stay here forever."

He grinned at her. "Eat your cereal."

"I will."

By the time she'd swallowed the last bite Kiko came along on Sancho. Amy shot out the door, got on behind Kiko, and Sancho's hoofs pattered along in a quick running walk. He was in a hurry.

"I have some things," said Kiko, and handed her a paper sack. It was full of rolled barley. "Easy to take it this way, some every day. Looks like our lunches. Mia needs lots to eat now. I have wire cutters, too," he added proudly, "and baling wire."

Amy wondered about that and waited.

"We don't want to make a plain trail through the wire gate," Kiko explained, and guided Sancho along the fence through the brush some distance from the gate.

He slid off, cut the wires by a post that was not far from another post, let Sancho and Amy through. He made a loop at the end of each wire, fastened baling wire to the loop, wrapped the baling wire around the fence post. "Now we have our own secret gate for Sancho, where no one will notice. We have to always be careful."

Sancho brayed with delight as they neared the corral. Mia whinnied an answer, and the colt, in a shrill little voice, said "He-he-he!" He stood as tall as he could, staring at them, his muscles held tight in the manner of new foals when they see something interesting.

They turned Sancho loose to graze and drink as he chose. He didn't need to be tied here now; nothing could drive him away. The colt became shy and hid behind his mother as they entered the corral, but very soon he was curious about them and unafraid.

He poked at them with his nose as they sat in the grass, pawed with his front hoof, tasted one of Amy's braids. When he lay down they could pet him all they wanted, feeling the curve of his neck, letting their hands follow his haunches, cupping his tiny hoofs. Where the earth was bare they noticed his tracks, each no bigger than a fifty-cent piece.

"Already he looks fuller, getting more round," observed Amy. "And he holds his neck so curved and proud when he walks. He's a little rocking-horse."

"If you pet a colt a lot on its first day, then it doesn't get scared of you later," Kiko explained. "When they stay out in pasture all the time with their mothers, then it's hard to get near them."

That day the colt practised running a little and kicking up his heels. Kiko tied Sancho to a bush so that he wouldn't come crowding around and so make Mia nervous. He led Mia to the pool, the colt jogging beside her. Mia drank, dribbled drops of cold water on him, and he laid his ears back and didn't like it. He dipped down his nose and tasted the water and let it run out of his mouth, then blew fluttering breaths at it.

Sancho, wanting to touch the colt, grew excited and pulled at his rope and pawed with an impatient front hoof. Mia, all protective now, put back her ears and glared at him. She had been glad to have his company before she had foaled, but now she considered him potential danger.

She was watchful and suspicious, imagining hungry mountain lions behind every tree and boulder, feeling sure that every stick might be a snake. Later, when the colt grew older, she would be Sancho's friend again, but now she would let no one but Amy and Kiko near.

The colt slept for some minutes, lying with his head in Amy's lap, Kiko lying close beside him, Mia standing guard. Amy liked to smell his warm coat, it was so good, and Mia must have thought so too, for she was constantly nosing him.

Everyone was so quiet that the birds came near, and a mother ground squirrel, with three young ones, came to eat the grains of barley that Mia had spilled. The young squirrels were at a gangly, spindly age but as quick and bright-eyed as their mother, and a soft woodsy brown.

The big oaks and the wild flowers, blue sky, white clouds, green grass, and even the beautiful mountains far away all seemed friendly and a part of the secret.

Amy smiled happily to herself and wondered what they'd name the colt.

She heard Kiko speaking to him in Spanish. She was fascinated. "What are you saying?"

"Don't you know?" asked Kiko, astonished.

"How could I?"

"Don't you know the Spanish?"

"Of course not."

Kiko shook his head in bewilderment. He had assumed that everyone knew Spanish.

"What is that word you said?" Amy persisted.

"*Tesoro.*"

She repeated the word and liked it. "What does it mean?"

Kiko had to stop and search for the English word. "Let's see. Tesoro. Golly, something like being rich." He scratched his head. "I guess it means treasure."

"Tesoro. Treasure. We could name him that. He *is* a treasure. Tesoro sounds good. It says 'soar,' too, like a horse soaring over a jump. I like that."

"It's all right. He's like a little deer, too."

"What would that word be?"

"*Ciervo,*" suggested Kiko.

"What's a baby deer, a fawn?"

"Let's see now. That would be *Cervato.*"

"He looks a little like a rabbit."

"*Conejo,*" said Kiko.

"Those are all nice names. What do you think, Kiko?"

"Tesoro is all right."

"Tesoro," repeated Amy. "His nickname could be Soro."

"*Zorro* is the fox."

Amy looked at the colt lovingly. "He *is* a treasure," she repeated.

The colt was all twitches and wiggles, never still, not even when he slept. Deep in dreams, he jerked his feet and whinnied, moved his lips as if feasting on some delicious dream food. When he was awake he was always bobbing his little head, twitching his ears,

67

stamping at flies, switching his tail, galloping about. Sometimes he reared straight up to paw the air, sometimes he kicked up his heels, practicing to be a bronco. Occasionally he kicked his mother.

The play of baby animals has to do with the conditions the animal will meet in its adult life. When Tesoro ran he was learning to run from danger. When he bucked and pitched, nature was showing him how to defend himself from a lion. When he reared high and struck with sharp front hoofs, he was dispensing with some enemy. And all the while he was getting valuable exercise and having fun besides.

He was filled with confidence, as are all baby animals. He was positive that his mother would always be near, ready to feed him and protect him, that she would never let anything unpleasant happen to him. The world he knew was friendly and safe.

The children were completely in love with him. It was unthinkable that if they had not brought Mia to this place Tesoro would not be in existence at all. He might not have been allowed even one hour of life on a shining April afternoon. Mia, in whom he had such confidence, would not have been able to save him, though she would have been frantic with worry and fear and grief.

The children could not in the least understand why a colt should not be allowed its life. Kiko was positive that when he grew up to be a man he would never be like some of the grownups he knew.

10

THE SATURDAY THAT Tesoro was two weeks old, Kiko produced a tiny colt halter. "Where did you get it?" Amy asked.

"Out of the tack room. I did not steal it, only borrowed it."

In the midst of petting Tesoro, Kiko slipped the halter on and buckled it. Tesoro shook his head. This thing did not shake off. It didn't really bother him and soon he forgot to fuss about it.

Two weeks had made a difference in his size and appearance and way of going. He had grown round, and all of him was a series of curves. His neck curved into his chest, his rump curved into his hind legs, his little belly curved.

Just as Kiko had predicted, his ankles had strengthened and he no longer walked with his hoofs pointing skyward. He was a strong little being and felt mighty. He romped and played and swaggered. He had teeth and bit at the grass, even nibbled at his mother's rolled barley. His coat was soft and his kinky mane and tail were very black. In little spots where his mouse-colored hair was beginning to shed, his new black coat was showing. His eyes were set well apart, giving him a knowing look, and his ears were always pricked up with interest.

He loved the children, as if he realized that they too were young things. Usually, when he saw them coming he said "He-he-he!" Already he liked a race, and sometimes Kiko and Amy stayed outside the corral to run along the fence. Then Tesoro raced up and down the fence line, with sudden kickings up of his heels, and much putting of his head down between his front legs while he gave terrific bucks. He felt that he knew exactly how to be a bronco.

But this day when he was two weeks old was, as Kiko said, to be his first day of school. "He is almost too young, but he is little and we are bigger than he is. Soon he will be bigger and stronger than we are. So now it is a good time to teach him something."

Kiko sat in the grass and when Tesoro bent down his head to him Kiko snapped the end of a lead rope into the halter ring.

Tesoro didn't notice at first, but when he started to move away he felt the restraint, and, as Kiko stood up, Tesoro pulled back. He could not free himself, so he all but sat on his haunches and pulled vigorously, his body swaying from side to side. Kiko stood firmly and let him pull.

Mia looked anxious and hurried to touch him with her nose.

70

Finally, Tesoro went straight up on his hind legs, then moved forward as he came down on his little front hoofs. That forward movement made the rope slack so that he did not feel the pull, and he took a step toward Kiko. Kiko petted him.

But again he wanted to move away and couldn't, and again he pulled and fought. Again, accidently, he came forward, and when he came forward he felt no restraint and was petted. Soon he did not mind about the rope. His mother was there, Kiko and Amy, who had never hurt him, and the rope seemed to be a part of the way things were in this mysterious business of living.

When Tesoro had arrived at this opinion, Kiko said, "This is enough school for today," and unsnapped the rope. "Tomorrow we will try again."

They let him wear the halter until it was time for them to hurry home. "He might get it caught on something," said Kiko, and took it off and hid it under the sheltering boulders where they stored the hay and grain.

To the children's amusement, Tesoro did what any grown horse, freshly unsaddled and turned free, would do. He plopped down and took a good roll, over and back and over, his four hoofs flourishing themselves at the sky.

"You'd think he just got ridden ten, twenty miles," said Kiko admiringly.

Whenever possible, after dark, Kiko filled sacks with hay, took them to be hidden in the brush by the trail into the canyon. Then, when they went again, Sancho packed two feeds of good oat hay to Mia's own private hay barn sheltered by boulders on the mountain.

As Amy was discovering, there was a great deal of work and plan-

71

ning connected with this business of keeping Mia and her colt in a safe place. But Tesoro was worth any amount of work and worry.

Amy's mother sometimes wondered why no carrot, apple, or lump of sugar stayed long in the house. Bread disappeared, sometimes half a loaf at a time.

The next day Tesoro wore his halter and rope again. When he had ceased to complain about the rope, Kiko said, "Now we will teach him some more." He put a rope on Mia and handed it to Amy. "You walk along and lead her."

Kiko walked beside Amy, and at first Tesoro did not realize that he was being led, he thought he was walking free by his mother's side. Then he discovered the restraint of the rope and braced his four hoofs. Kiko pulled sideways on the rope, which threw him off balance and prevented him from standing firmly. "Like a little mule," Kiko observed.

Tesoro had to step, which brought him forward, which in turn brought forth a reward. The children praised him. Soon he allowed himself to be led beside Mia.

But when Kiko suggested to Amy, "Now just stand still with Mia," Tesoro objected to being led away. Again his hoofs braced themselves, again he nearly sat down. "Come," said Kiko, pulling to the side, making Tesoro step. But the colt didn't want to be led all around unless he could walk beside Mia.

"Just drop her rope," Kiko ordered. "Get behind Tesoro and push him a little. If I didn't have anyone to help me I'd put a loop over his rump and pull on that rope while I pulled on his halter rope. That would be the same as if he was being pushed. My father can break colts to lead that way."

Mia watched them but didn't worry. Her colt didn't seem to be in any great trouble. What with Kiko giving little tugs on the rope and Amy pushing mightily, Tesoro got the idea.

"He's very smart," Amy observed as Tesoro became so willing that Kiko could lead him back and forth and all around the corral.

"You take him around once and then we'll turn him loose. Run a little and see if he'll trot up behind you."

Tesoro had his lesson learned. When the rope told him to come faster he broke into a lively little up-and-down trot.

"That's good," Kiko approved. "Now pet him and unsnap the rope. We'll lead him a little every day so's he won't forget, and next we'll teach him to let us pick up his feet. Only I guess someday we ought to teach them both to stake out. It would come in handy."

"Stake out?"

"So they could graze on a long rope like Sancho does, without getting tangled up and rope-burned. Then we could tie them to graze wherever we could find a spot of good grass. Of course Tesoro wouldn't leave Mia anyway, but he ought to know about a long rope. My father says every horse should learn to be staked."

"We ought to lead him, just for the practice, when we take Mia to the spring."

"Yes, that's good."

Always before they left, they took Mia for a last drink. Kiko had removed another water bucket from the ranch and now two buckets were left full when Kiko and Amy had to go home. Very often Tesoro managed to upset one or both. Kiko planned to figure a way to wire the buckets to the fence so neither could be upset. He was thinking

73

of hot, thirsty days ahead.

Sancho still had to be caught and tied when Mia and her colt went to the spring. He could scarcely endure not being allowed to touch the colt, but Mia was firm of the opinion that no other animal should come near her child.

Sancho had eyes like bright beads staring out from under the thick gray of his brow. His long soft ears went straight up with attention, he pawed with a foreleg and pulled at his rope. Mia put her ears back flat and glared at him.

"Poor Sancho," Amy told him. "But someday Mia won't care." Amy loved Sancho, who usually seemed so wise and so patient. Certainly Kiko had no need of toys such as city children owned. Sancho was a live plaything and the very best.

Now Sancho watched yearningly as they led the colt to the spring. Tesoro liked to drink water now too, and this sunny afternoon he did more than drink, he struck at the water with a playful front hoof, splashed cold drops on his belly and jumped straight into the air.

"*Payaso!*" Kiko said when he could stop laughing.

"What does that mean?"

"It means he is a clown."

This day they led mare and colt around the clearing before they put them back in the corral and sat down to admire them. They never grew tired of staring at Tesoro, his little sun-warmed body was so beautiful.

Kiko pointed out, "When he gets as big as Mia he'll be worth money."

Amy took a sudden look at the future and was bewildered. She had been so happy about the colt that she hadn't thought ahead.

74

"But whose money, Kiko? They aren't really ours, we didn't steal them even. We only hid them." A frightening thought assailed her. "Probably they really belong to Mr. Richie."

Kiko shrugged. "Who knows?" He was very good at planning what should happen from day to day, but a long view of this problem was too baffling and he'd given it no consideration. "Well, they're all right for now," he said, "and later we can think of something."

"Like what?"

"Oh, I don't know. But something."

11

Came the glad day when it was vacation time at last and all the
land was solid gold. Amy, accustomed to living in a summer-green
country, had thought that she would not like the dry season. Now she
was astonished at all the color in the tawny hills, at how vivid were
tree leaves, at the different shades of green.

With no hope of rain, a number of wild flowers kept right on
blooming. It was all a magic land to Amy, and Tesoro was the most
enchanting creature in it.

"What is Tesoro's father like?" she asked Kiko.

"Not bad. He's a gelding now and he's bigger. He's my cousin's horse. They never planned to keep him for a stallion anway. It took him a long time to grow and look good because his mother died before he got enough milk. They ride him now. He's all right."

"Let's go over to the reservation some day and see him."

"Uh-huh."

Kiko was being thoughtful lately and spending a great deal of time brushing and petting Mia, almost ignoring Tesoro. One day he produced something, a sort of nose band with a head stall, which he put on Mia. There were rope reins.

"What's that?"

"Oh, a hackamore I picked up."

"What's a hackamore?"

"You can see. Like a bridle, only different. No bit. They break the quarter horses with them."

"You mean you'll break Mia to ride?"

"Why not? She's over two years old now and tall and strong. And we're light."

"But how do you know how to do everything?"

"Oh, I watch the men. And my father tells me lots of things. My father is one good vaquero. Here, I will let you help me. What we really need are long lines, to get in back and drive her with. That's the way they do it but I was afraid to take any. So we'll do it this way. I will walk by Mia's neck and I will teach her to neck rein, by pulling this way and that. All you have to do is walk in back of her and cluck at her when she stops going. Unless I tell her to stop; that is when I say *whoa* and pull back."

Kiko could turn Mia to the left easily because he walked on that side, but he was not tall and she was, so he could not reach to pull the reins to the right. When he could keep her going in a straight line, make her stop when he pulled back, make her turn to the left, he switched and walked on the right side of her.

Every day he walked with her, turning her this way and that, feeling more and more eager to get on her and see what she would do.

By this time Mia was completely accustomed to having the children around and under her. They leaned on her, they had petted and brushed every spot of her, she wasn't likely to feel any alarm at the slight weight of either of them.

When he was three months old, in July, Tesoro had arrived at that magic time in a colt's life when he showed precisely how he would look two years later. He was a perfectly proportioned small horse. As he continued growing he would, for a time, lose that appearance, he would grow leggy again, be unproportioned, look gangling. But now he was smooth and even and beautiful, shining black all over. He had a fat little rump, which the children spanked frequently, and he didn't care. Kiko knew that from the time a colt is born it must be accustomed to having its rump petted as well as its nose, for then it will not be inclined to kick.

Mia wore an aristocratic look. She was well fed and fat but there was no appearance of heaviness about her. She looked as if she could gallop cross country and fly over fences and never be tired.

Instead of being ridden under an English saddle and working with a snaffle bit, Mia was being trained to rein like a Western horse because Kiko had a hackamore and thought this was the easiest way to do the job anyhow. He'd seen quarter horses being trained, but the hunters went to Mr. Richie's other ranch for training. He wasn't

78

doing this exactly as the men did, anyway, but he was doing it the best way he could figure.

He wanted to have some control over Mia before he tried riding her, he wanted her to know how to turn and how to stop. Especially how to stop. He didn't relish the thought of Mia suddenly becoming excited and taking off on her long legs at a fast run to anywhere.

Mia accepted Sancho again, after the colt had grown past what she considered the helpless stage. She permitted Tesoro and Sancho to stand together, chewing lovingly on each other's necks. Tesoro made the children laugh when first he was allowed to approach Sancho, for he moved his jaws vigorously, chewing the air in Sancho's direction. This is a thing all colts do upon meeting a stranger, but no one knows why.

Now Tesoro admired Sancho above and beyond anything. It was as if he planned on growing to be strong and wise like his friend Sancho. And Sancho appeared to be as fond of the colt as Mia was. Sancho was not very big, but he was larger than Tesoro, and he treated his little friend gently, even when Tesoro reached to bite his long ears.

On a hot July day when Tesoro and Sancho were standing head to tail, switching each other's flies, and Mia was feeling unruffled, Kiko decided that now was the time. He put a lead rope around Mia's neck, slipped on the hackamore, led her alongside a big boulder, and scrambled up on the boulder.

"Now," he said to Amy, "you lead her around, walk straight until I say 'turn left' or 'turn right,' and when I say 'whoa,' you stop, too."

He slid from the boulder to Mia's back, petted her neck and shoulders and talked to her while she, unalarmed, stood quietly. After

79

all, a horse bucks for three reasons only—it is frightened, or it feels playful, or it really wants to remove its rider and goes about it in the most efficient way. Mia was not feeling playful this warm day, she was not frightened, and she had no reason to want Kiko to get off her. There was no saddle, no tight cinch to make her uncomfortable.

"Okay," said Kiko. He picked up his rope reins and started moving Mia. She walked solemnly around the clearing, turning right and left as the reins told her to. There seemed to be no problem at all.

12

"A MAN IS HERE," Kiko told Amy worriedly.

"A man?"

"Yes. My father told me. Some cousin of Mr. Richie's."

"What is he going to do?"

"Look for Mia, I guess."

"Look for Mia? Kiko, I'm scared!"

"Me too."

"Where's Mr. Richie?"

"He's away somewhere and this man, he's staying in Mr. Richie's house."

"Well, we'll have to be more careful than ever."

But what further precautions they could take Amy didn't know. They never left a plain trail anywhere. They wound cautiously through the brush and the only place they left tracks was at Black Horse Spring in Black Horse Canyon where they let it be known they went to play. If the man were going to be snooping about everywhere, it was going to be more difficult to haul the feed down the canyon and up the mountain.

They worried steadily that day all the way to Mia and Tesoro. When they reached the hiding place Amy felt more confident. "I don't see how he could find this spot. Not even the cowboys could, not even your father, and he knows this country."

But Kiko was pessimistic. If the man didn't know the country, then he wouldn't have sense enough to know which place would be an unlikely place to look. Not being a cowboy, the man might not think about following tracks; the fact that the wire gate below the brushy trail looked unused might not keep him from going through it.

This seemed too involved to explain and Kiko shrugged his shoulders. He said helplessly, "Well, he might just ride around and look everywhere."

"What did your father say about him? Is he a city man or what?"

"I guess from the city. I don't know."

"And he can ride a horse?"

"I guess so."

"But not well?"

"How do I know?"

"I was thinking—" Amy frowned and stared across the hills and canyons. She loved the view from the corral on the mountain side

82

where, on toward Mexico, it seemed as if tall mountains were peering eagerly over the shoulders of lower hills. But now she was noting only that all the country appeared wild and rough and difficult to explore. "He won't know how to find his way around, will he?"

Kiko shook his head. "My father and all them don't think Mia's anywhere around here. They think she got hauled off in a truck or trailer." He jumped on Sancho. "You wait here. I want to ride up the mountain, there's that look-out place. After this, one of us ought to watch a lot from up there. For if maybe he comes."

Amy sat down in the corral. Tesoro came to nose her, but she scarcely bothered to pet him she was so busy thinking. She didn't believe the man would be looking this soon, anyway, if he had just got to the ranch. They must plan on a course of action before he started wandering around too much.

Suddenly Sancho and Kiko reappeared. Kiko was wild-eyed. "Some one is coming, almost to the wire gate! A man on a horse. Jump on Sancho, quick. We got to head him off somehow."

Sancho had to jog downhill, a thing which he detested. He could hurry up a hill more easily than he could hurry down one, but insistent drumming on his sides from Kiko's heels kept him at it. To break into a lope he would not, not downhill.

At their secret opening in the fence both children jumped off and began unwinding wires. They yanked Sancho through, hooked up the wire, circled through the brush, and, urging Sancho into a lope, headed toward the wire gate.

They crashed out of a clump of brush and startled a horse on which a man was sitting. The horse whirled to snort at Sancho and the man sailed off.

83

"Oh, my!" Amy exclaimed, shocked and frightened. This was an unfortunate way to meet Mr. Richie's cousin.

Kiko wasted no time staring at the man on the ground. He leaped off Sancho and grabbed the man's horse by the reins. The horse, his nerves unsettled, was ready to leave the scene and hurry home.

The man sat up. "Do you always explode out of the bushes like that?" he asked angrily.

"Oh, dear," Amy apologized in a trembling voice. "We're sorry. We didn't mean to scare your horse. We didn't know anyone was here. Oh, I hope you aren't hurt."

"Look," Kiko observed. "Your glasses didn't even fall off."

The man put his hand to his face. "So they didn't," he said, seeming cheered about this.

"I don't know how you ever kept them on," Amy told him. "I'm sure I couldn't be thrown and keep glasses on."

"I caught your horse for you, too, and that's real lucky because he could have run home and left you on foot." Kiko looked pleased with himself.

The man began to feel better-natured. "Makes me feel like a fool to come a cropper."

Amy said quickly, "We fall off the burro all the time. But it's not such a long way to fall. Do you think you are hurt?"

Gingerly the man got to his feet. He wasn't very tall, he was slightly fat, and he had a pink complexion. His pale eyes blinked earnestly through his glasses. "I guess I'm all right. A little stiff, though." He hobbled toward his horse. Amy picked up his hat and handed it to him.

"That's a funny-looking saddle," Kiko remarked.

"An English saddle," Amy explained, for the first time able to inform Kiko about something having to do with horses. "The kind they ride back East. The kind Mr. Richie's hunters would wear."

"It does look odd on a chunky quarter horse," the man agreed. "But it's my own saddle, I ride it a lot. And it's more comfortable than a Western so I brought it with me on my vacation."

"Vacation?" Amy asked.

"Yes, I get two weeks away from my job every year. I like to ride and my cousin's been urging me to come down here. He told me about the mare he'd lost and I thought I'd spend the time riding around looking for her. I ride quite a bit at home, at riding stables, of course. I thought I'd enjoy this and perhaps make some discovery to help Mr. Richie too. I'm staying in the big house while he's away."

"Kiko and I have looked and looked for Mia. That's the mare's name—she was our favorite. This is Kiko and I am Amy."

"And I'm Mr. Brothers, and not exactly delighted to meet you; I mean not the violent way we met." He smiled to show that he wasn't cross any more.

Amy smiled her friendliest smile. "Maybe we can make up for it. We could show you around. How did you happen to find the trail down the canyon to this old gate?"

"So this is a gate? I was wondering how it worked."

Kiko stared at him in amazement. "It's just a old gate. Like any gate. You push it out of the top loop of wire and out of the bottom."

"But no one's used it in a long time," Amy explained hastily.

85

"When Mia first got stolen we went through and looked. But no one had been on the mountain, it's too rough. Perhaps once there was a trail, but now it's all thick brush and big rocks. We couldn't find a thing."

"Oh. Well. Anyway, I was only riding around to get used to the horse and the lay of the land. It was just a thought I had that the mare could be hidden somewhere, or that she got loose and would be wandering about."

"That's what we thought at first. But then they decided she must have been hauled off to somewhere. But we still look for her when we don't have anything else to do."

Mr. Brothers nodded. "I feel I've had enough for today." Awkwardly, feeling stiff and battered, he climbed on his horse.

"Guess we'll go home, too," Kiko said.

"We'll ride along with you," Amy offered. "That is, if you don't mind."

"Sure, come ahead. That's a cute little donkey. Can he keep up with a horse?"

"Golly, yes," Kiko assured him.

"We ride him all over everywhere," Amy said. "His name is Sancho."

Mr. Brothers thought that these were nice children and that they might be helpful since they seemed to know the country so well.

13

K<small>IKO AND</small> A<small>MY</small> shuddered every time they thought about Mr. Brothers coming directly to the wire gate. Had he passed through, he could easily have found their trail through the tall brush. In a short time he could have discovered Mia and Tesoro. All this on his very first day of riding around and looking! Pleasant as he was, Mr. Brothers was a very dangerous man.

"What we have to do is watch him all the time," Kiko announced.

"But how can we and take care of Mia and Tesoro?"

Kiko sighed and scratched his head.

Amy thought that perhaps, since they'd headed Mr. Brothers off

87

once, he wouldn't look again in the same direction. But Kiko didn't feel safe about it; the man might be curious enough to come back and try the gate again. He might be more suspicious than he had appeared.

"We could watch a lot from the look-out place," Amy suggested.

Kiko shook his head. "If we hurried and headed him off again like we did, it would look funny. He'd wonder."

"And I suppose it wouldn't do any good, if we saw him about to come, to take Mia and Tesoro into the brush. Even he could look at the corral and see that it's being used."

Kiko nodded. "By golly, the only way to do is to keep showing him around. Like you and Sancho go with him and I go feed the mare and colt. Some days you go feed and I'll ride with him."

"Wouldn't he think that was funny? That we didn't both ride Sancho as we usually do?"

"Well, we could say that we didn't like to ride Sancho double on real long rides. Or something. Anyway, we got to watch him. If we are both at the corral one of us has got to be at the look-out all the time. We'll have to haul feed after dark or before morning. I guess everything's got to be a lot more work now," Kiko added drearily.

"Maybe he'll give up and go away pretty soon."

Kiko had a happy thought. "You know that horse they gave him to ride? His name is Rojo. That means red, because he is a real red sorrel. Well, my father nor none of them ride him very much. He's real good, got a quick rein on him, but he's a bother to ride because he's jumpy. No one ever falls off him, but when someone's busy, like cutting out cows from calves, or trying to head off a cow that needs doctoring, or goes to rope something, why, this Rojo, he might shy

88

at a rabbit. You got to have a horse that keeps his mind on the cows and isn't going to jump at things when you're working him. So that's why they let Mr. Brothers have him to ride; they got others they like better."

"Oh, that's why he threw him there by the gate."

"Yes. And with that funny flat saddle Rojo can jump out from under Mr. Brothers awful quick." Kiko looked pleased.

Amy giggled. "That's mean. But, gee, we could have fun."

"The cowboys thinks it's funny too, my father says. They laugh about Mr. Brothers and how he makes himself go up and down on that saddle when Rojo trots. They say one time while he's up Rojo's not going to be there when he comes down. I think I better be the first to show him around. I know some good places."

"But I don't want to walk all the way to Mia and Tesoro."

"We did it all the time at first, when we kept Sancho there, before Mia had the colt."

"It was cooler then."

"Okay. We can all start off together and you can ride as far as Black Horse Spring. Then you want to get off and play there, and I'll take Mr. Brothers up on the ridge over toward the big canyon or somewheres. And sometimes we can both go on the burro; start Mr. Brothers off in some direction and tell him of some little canyon to look into or something. We can say we have to be home early and can't go all the way. Get him headed the wrong way and then we can hurry to Mia."

Amy reflected that Kiko was very good at planning and plotting. She remembered how, at the very first, she had had to try to plan how to rescue Mia and the unborn while Kiko had thought the

89

whole thing impossible. As soon as they had taken the first step Kiko kept thinking of how to do things. Now he had numbers of ideas as to how to deal best with Mr. Brothers.

Though he wore a wide-brimmed hat, Mr. Brothers became sunburned past the point of comfort. And though in Los Angeles, where he lived, he rode a couple of hours a week, it was along a gentle bridle trail in the park and was not enough riding to get certain muscles accustomed to this form of exercise. He wasn't used to being ready to duck from low limbs and stiff brush that reached for him, vegetation that bumped and scratched him. The weather was too hot, but he didn't complain for he liked to think of himself as an outdoor man and a horseman.

In spite of everything, he liked the wide and beautiful country through which the children guided him. Sometimes, when they rode not too far, both children went with him. He liked them and admired the ease with which they traveled rough trails and the way they knew their way around the hills. They had quick eyes so that it was seldom that Mr. Brothers was the first to see a deer or coyote.

Amy liked the fact that Mr. Brothers was interested in the wild creatures, that he agreed with her that it couldn't be fun to shoot at something as beautiful as a deer.

"I like birds and animals better alive," he told her.

He was a bird watcher, too, and carried field glasses. He knew more about the birds and their names than the children did.

Amy liked him so much that she was sincerely sorry for every one of his disasters.

If Mr. Brothers stared at a bird, Kiko found a low-hanging branch to ride under and, before he knew it, Mr. Brothers was in trouble. Rojo jumped at the sight of Mr. Brothers' hat coming to earth and Mr. Brothers followed his hat.

Mr. Brothers didn't always get thrown, but sometimes he came so near to it that it was wildly exciting. Once he managed to stay on when he was so far off-balance that arms and legs were going like windmills. Often he himself nearly turned Rojo out from under him because he was unaccustomed to riding so well-reined a horse. He had to remember that Rojo would respond instantly.

"It's a good thing we go with you, to catch Rojo after you fall off," Kiko remarked.

"But you don't fall off nearly so much as at first," Amy said encouragingly.

Another problem of Mr. Brothers' was his saddle. A Western saddle, preferably one built with a quarter-horse spread, would have fitted Rojo better. The English saddle that would have looked well on one of the long-legged hunters was all wrong for Rojo. His withers wouldn't hold it back when he went down a steep hill, and Mr. Brothers nearly went over his head.

Rojo's round back was such that if Mr. Brothers mounted without putting enough spring into his ascent, the saddle turned toward him. It had to be readjusted and tightened and fussed with a dozen times on every ride. Finally, Mr. Brothers gave up, got off, walked, and led his horse down every steep trail.

At last he said, "I don't see any point in all this. We just ride aimlessly around on all sorts of crazy trails."

"But where do you want to look?" asked Amy. "We don't know any better than you do where would be a good place to look."

91

Kiko offered, "Tomorrow I'll take you over on the rim of the big deep canyon. My father said that years ago cattle rustlers would hide a whole bunch of cows down there. I never been down in there, but I'll ask my father where the trail goes. It's pretty rough, I think."

"Did anyone look down there for the mare?"

"I don't think so. I don't know."

"I want to go, too, if my mother will let me," Amy said.

Later, when they were alone, Kiko said she couldn't go. "We might be gone all day and you had better go see to the mare and colt. Besides, I have a plan."

"What sort of plan?" Amy wanted to know.

"You'll see."

"Well, I wish I could go."

"How do you think you can? I am the one who knows about the big canyon, and my father can tell me about the trail. Who is going to look after the mare and colt if we both go?"

Amy had to agree.

The next day she rode with them as far as Black Horse Spring and announced her intention of staying there as it was too hot to be riding up over the ridge and on to the great canyon. A little wistfully, she watched Mr. Brothers and Kiko ride on, but then it was not exactly a hardship to go to Mia and Tesoro, tend to their feed and water, and play with Tesoro awhile.

She didn't see Kiko until the next morning. He was elated. "Mr. Brothers won't be going with us for a couple of days. He's got poison oak and he doesn't feel so good."

"Oh, Kiko! You must have taken him right through some."

"Well, I didn't know he gets it. I never catch it. You don't either."

92

"But you thought perhaps he might."

"Uh huh."

Lying in misery on his bed, his face so swollen that his eyes were useless for reading, Mr. Brothers had time to ponder.

It occurred to him that these children might not be as guileless as they appeared. Every time he rode with them he had some stupid kind of mishap and, though they appeared dismayed and sympathetic, it might be that they were being crafty instead.

He realized that for some time he had been getting the impression that they knew more than they were willing to disclose.

14

"THEY MUST WATCH me very closely," Mr. Brothers thought a few days later, as he was over by the barn putting his saddle on Rojo. He had never planned with the children at what hour they'd ride but whenever he went after his horse, one or the other or both showed up on the burro.

Now the two came along and Amy said, "That must have been an awful dose of poison oak. The only time I ever had it I just had a tiny itchy place."

"You feel good now?" asked Kiko brightly.

"Yes, I feel good. But you know, I'm tired of you kids leading

94

me on. What sort of wild-goose chase do you plan on for today?"

They were taken aback. Finally Amy said, "What do you mean?"

"I think you know."

Kiko looked frightened and Amy was ready to cry.

"But we don't know," she protested.

"You do. You know something about that mare you aren't telling. Do you realize you could get into very serious trouble?"

They stared at him with stricken eyes.

Mr. Brothers' hand shot out and gripped Kiko's shoulder. He gave Kiko a hard shake. Kiko looked completely astonished and helpless.

"Listen! I liked you children. I though you were my friends. Let's talk this over now. Tell me exactly what you've been up to."

Amy looked at Kiko and Kiko looked at Amy.

Amy cleared her throat, tried to control her trembling.

"Mr. Brothers, did you know that Mia was going to have a colt?"

"No, I didn't."

"Well, when she was much too young she got with a little stallion on the Indian reservation and Mr. Richie was furious. He thought she'd have just an impossible scrub colt and he was going to shoot it when it was born. He thought the stallion was dreadful-looking, and he thought that perhaps he'd have to have Mia shot, too, because having a colt when she was so young, she might never develop well and grow and be worth money. Kiko and I thought that was terrible and we couldn't let it be that way."

Kiko stared at Amy as a man would stare at a traitor. "Shut up," he commanded.

Mr. Brothers was looking sympathetic. "Go on, Amy," he said

kindly.

Amy took a deep shuddering breath. "So Kiko and I didn't know what to do. We couldn't have a new baby colt killed. Could you, Mr. Brothers?"

"No. I wouldn't like that. But Mr. Richie had his reasons."

"So," said Amy, almost happily, "Kiko has cousins on the reservation and Kiko knows all the Indians. So we told the Indians. And they didn't like a colt to be killed either. And it was right after that Mia vanished."

Mr. Brothers was too interested in Amy's words to notice the sudden relief on Kiko's face.

She continued, "The Indians would never tell us anything because of course it wouldn't be safe for us to know, in case we got asked a lot of questions. But Kiko and I think for sure that somewhere on the reservation Mia lives with a dear little colt."

Kiko finally came to his senses. "But we didn't want you going over there and looking. So we took you riding all kinds of other places. We don't want them to find Mia and kill her colt. Do you?"

"Hum," said Mr. Brothers. "Well. I didn't know about any unwanted colt to be born. My cousin didn't mention that."

"I hope you won't tell Mr. Richie what we told you," Amy begged. "He hates Indians anyway."

"Well, certainly I won't tell him now. But I think I will go look around."

Amy said quickly, "But we don't want the Indians to get into trouble. And we don't want the colt killed. Oh, Mr. Brothers, you shouldn't have made us tell."

Mr. Brothers looked rueful. "I almost wish I hadn't started this.

96

Well, anyway, I'm going to ride the reservation."

He got on Rojo and Kiko moved Sancho beside him.

"Oh no," said Mr. Brothers. "No. This time you fellows aren't coming. I'm tired of being taken under low branches and through poison oak. I'm sick and tired of falling off this horse. No. Now you stay home like good little children and I'll let you know when I find anything."

For some days thereafter the Indians were treated to the entertaining sight of Mr. Brothers posting along on the chunky quarter horse. They enjoyed this enormously.

"At least I have a lead," Mr. Brothers thought as, doggedly, he followed the reservation trails and roadways. He had the uncomfortable, ear-burning sensation that he was being watched, that even when he went through one of those odd-looking wire gates and found his way into some remote canyon or meadow, he was being observed. Dogs barked at him as he passed houses, small children stared at him, but he seldom saw an adult. This really didn't matter as it would do no good to question anyone, anyway.

He saw cattle and he saw horses but he saw no mare that answered the description he had of Mia. He felt frustrated and he was tired of riding under the hot sun. He thought of what Amy had told him of the foal and decided he didn't like his cousin, Carver Richie, very much. But now that he had started this search he didn't like to give up.

He didn't know what to think of this business of the mare getting bred too young and having a colt. Perhaps the mare, after the Indians took her, had died foaling.

Without the children along, Mr. Brothers didn't have so many misadventures. He was careful about the trails he followed, he remembered to sit tight in case Rojo took it into his head to shy at some rabbit or squirrel. He didn't let his hat get brushed off and he didn't look at birds through his field glasses unless he dismounted first.

It made him unhappy to think that the children whom he had liked and trusted had been having fun at his expense. They had seemed to be simple, honest children while all the time they were being sly and deceitful.

Suddenly he thought, "They could still be lying!"

He stopped Rojo and sat meditating. If they had made up this story about the mare and the colt and the Indians, then it proved that the mare really was alive and they were protecting her. If they knew nothing whatever about the whereabouts of the animal, or animals, as the case might be, they wouldn't have needed to go to the trouble of giving him a bad time, they wouldn't have needed to tell that story.

"By Jove!" Mr. Brothers exclaimed, aloud and with such suddenness that Rojo gave a nervous start and nearly left him in mid-air.

"By Jove," he repeated, recovering his balance. "I think I've hit upon something now."

He turned and rode back the way he had come, concentrating on a plan of action. He realized that the children had not been letting him out of their sights until they thought that they had him safely sidetracked on the Indian reservation.

From now on he was going to do some detective work and not let the children out of *his* sight. He was nearly positive that they knew

98

exactly where the mare was, that they went to visit her from time to time.

He too could be sly, and the thought pleased him very much.

Amy said, as they rode slowly down Black Horse Canyon, "Why does Sancho keep putting one ear back?"

Kiko chuckled. "Don't you know?"

"No. Why?"

"Because we're being followed, that's why."

"But Kiko, who?"

"I guess Mr. Brothers. He must have got tired of the reservation."

"Oh, dear! What will we do?"

"That's easy. We'll just have to have some more fun. We'll let him follow us around and around through the brush and up steep hills and down steep hills and back and forth and home. He might even have to follow us through some poison oak. All we have to do is make enough noise so he won't lose the trail. We might even sing a little bit."

Amy giggled. But she said, "That's all right for now. But when we want to go to Mia, what then?"

"Oh, that's okay. One of us will keep on riding the burro and leaving clear tracks; and the other one, maybe me, will go crawling off through the brush. After Mr. Brothers rides by, I'll go to the mare and colt. He'll probably fall off Rojo—I could make him do it easy enough—or he'll get poison oak again, and we can go to the mountain whenever we like."

"But I thought he believed us. I thought he'd keep riding on the reservation."

99

"Now I guess he thinks he should follow us."

"That isn't good, Kiko. It means that he's suspicious of us after all."

Kiko stopped Sancho and looked at a narrow deer trail that started off into the brush. "We can try this if we wait awhile—until he catches up enough to see which way we go."

Riding slowly and cautiously, Mr. Brothers rounded a bend in time to see Sancho's wispy tail disappear into the brush. "Ah ha," he said to himself, and waited until he felt it safe to follow.

It was such a narrow, uncomfortable trail to ride that finally Mr. Brothers got off and led his horse. He was elated to discover that he could follow the burro's tracks quite well, and from time to time he could hear the children's voices.

The trail wound up to a ridge and from the ridge Mr. Brothers glimpsed the burro starting down into another canyon. He ducked out of sight behind some scrub oak so that if they chanced to look back they wouldn't see him. Carefully he emerged and stepped forward to watch the slow progress of Sancho down a steep slope. He waited, then, still walking, followed the tracks.

A deer crashed out of the brush and Rojo gave a nervous leap, bumped into Mr. Brothers and knocked him down. Mr. Brothers lost his glasses this time but managed to hold tight to the end of the reins so that Rojo couldn't desert him.

For some dreadful moments he thought he was going to go rolling down the steep hill, but Rojo saved him by being frightened of him in this odd position and pulling back to the end of the reins.

After that, Mr. Brothers had to search for his glasses, which was difficult for he did not see well without them. Fortunately, he found

100

them unbroken. He proceeded, not feeling as exultant as he had, and when he neared the floor of the canyon he glimpsed the children resting in the shade of a tree. This was lucky, for he feared that after all this delay they might have gone so far he couldn't pick up sight or track of them again.

However, it turned out to be a disappointing day, for, after journeying aimlessly around, seeming to ride in circles, and going through a great deal of thick and scratchy brush, the children ended up at home.

Mr. Brothers took a hot bath and observed that he had more than several black and blue marks, that his face and arms were scratched, that he felt stiff, sore, and completely tired. Disgustedly, he went to bed.

But he didn't go to sleep at once. His mind wouldn't quiet down. It kept wandering in as many circles as the children had taken him riding that day, and finally it ended up where he had begun his misadventures—right at the wire gate where first he had met Amy and Kiko.

Thinking back, he remembered how hastily he had been assured that there was nothing beyond the gate—only a mountain covered with brush and rocks where you couldn't go anywhere, where no one had been for a long time.

"Ah ha!" Mr. Brothers thought, and dropped happily off to sleep.

The next morning the children found Mr. Brothers over by the barn. He moved stiffly. He had a rope on Rojo and was using currycomb and brush.

"Thought I'd take another ride over on the reservation, but I don't

101

seem to be having much luck. Still, if I keep riding around I just might happen to find the mare and colt."

"Are you hurt?" Amy asked anxiously. "You seem to be limping."

"No, I guess I just rode too far yesterday."

They watched as he put on his funny flat saddle, and, groaning, climbed up. They watched as he took the road to the reservation. They waited some time after that to make sure he really meant to go there. When he didn't come back they started down the canyon.

Now Kiko was puzzled. "Why'd he go back over there for, when he'd decided he better follow us?"

"I guess yesterday made him decide not to follow us any more. Perhaps he thinks we don't know anything after all."

"Maybe not, but maybe so. We got to be careful anyway."

When they reached the corral Kiko didn't linger. "You feed and water, I'm going up to the look-out."

He returned almost at once. "Quick, get a rope on Mia! Get her and the colt out of the corral."

He turned Sancho into the corral, which pleased Sancho as Amy had just thrown in some hay. Kiko took off running, leading Mia. Tesoro scampered along behind and Amy ran to keep up. As fast as possible, they wound their way up through the brush and rocks. When they reached what seemed to be a safe and hidden place Kiko stopped and gasped for breath.

"Mr. Brothers was coming right through the wire gate," he panted. "He'll be at the corral any minute. I want him to think that's where we keep Sancho when we come to play on the mountain. Now you go back down and tell him something before he notices mare and colt tracks."

102

"Like it's our secret place and we didn't want anyone to find it?"

"Yes, or we are looking for treasure or something. Hurry. Head him off somehow."

There was Mr. Brothers, sitting on Rojo, staring at Sancho and the corral. With a little shriek, intended to express surprise, Amy burst out of the brush.

Rojo whirled, Mr. Brothers shot off and lay quietly with his head pillowed on a rock.

Remembering Kiko's quick action when Mr. Brothers had gone off at other times, Amy grabbed Rojo's reins and tied him to a bush. Then she hurried to peer down on the prone form of Mr. Brothers.

"Oh, dear!" she cried. "Please get up, Mr. Brothers! I don't want you to be hurt!"

But Mr. Brothers continued to rest peacefully.

"Kiko!" Amy screamed. "Kiko, come here, quick!"

She began to cry because poor Mr. Brothers looked so inactive. "Kiko, hurry!"

Finally, cautiously, Kiko emerged from the brush. He had taken care to tie Mia firmly to a scrub oak on the mountain and he didn't think Tesoro would wander far from her.

"Kiko! Look at Mr. Brothers. He won't wake up!"

Kiko stared earnestly at his fallen foe. "He's out colder than a codfish, but I think we can fix him."

He got Mia's water bucket, filled it with cold spring water, dumped it forcefully over Mr. Brothers' head. Sputtering, Mr. Brothers sat up.

"Oh!" he groaned.

"Oh!" Amy echoed. "I'm so glad! You're all right, Mr. Brothers? You're better now, aren't you?"

Mr. Brothers put his hand to his head and slowly sank to a reclining position again.

"You just got knocked out," Kiko explained. "You'll be all right in a few minutes."

"Oh, dear," Amy lamented. "This time your glasses really *are* broken. All in teensy pieces."

Mr. Brothers moaned.

"Don't sit up too fast," Kiko cautioned. "All you did was get knocked out. I seen lots of cowboys get knocked out worse than you." In his excitement Kiko was swiftly losing what grammar he had.

Carefully, slowly, Mr. Brothers sat up again. He felt his head.

"By golly, you got a knot," Kiko informed him admiringly. "I think maybe it's the biggest I ever did see."

Mr. Brothers felt it tenderly. "Must be a concussion," he said, and reached for Amy. She helped him to his feet and he swayed dizzily.

"You better sit down for a few minutes," Kiko suggested.

Mr. Brothers complied. "What happened?"

"I didn't mean to," Amy explained. "Honestly I didn't. I came out of the brush too quickly. I didn't know you were here and Rojo jumped out from under you."

Dazedly, Mr. Brothers recalled the reason for his being here. "What's all this corral and everything?"

"Where we come to play. It's our very own secret place. The hermit used to live here a long time ago. So we fixed up the corral to keep Sancho in so we can go climb around on the mountain. Mr. Brothers, can you keep a secret?"

Mr. Brothers wasn't very interested in secrets just then but he started to nod and instantly wished he hadn't.

104

Amy continued, "We think perhaps the hermit might have hidden some money around here. Like buried treasure, you know. We're searching for it. We never wanted anyone to know about this place so that's why we tried to keep you away. Mr. Brothers, really and truly we didn't want to make such trouble for you. I feel terrible."

Kiko was uneasy. What if Mia should grow tired of being tied, what if Tesoro should wander a little and she or he should whinny? What if Sancho should lose interest in his hay and start braying for them—and they'd answer?

"I think," Kiko suggested, "kind of slow we ought to go home. Amy, you bring Mr. Brothers a drink of water. Then we'll help him onto his horse."

Mr. Brothers looked at Rojo with distaste. Rojo appeared to be a red blur, as, without his glasses, Mr. Brothers had difficulty.

He asked, "Would you kids mind awfully if I rode the burro? He's not so tall and is easier to get on, and if I go to falling off again it wouldn't be so far down. Could you two ride Rojo?"

"Oh, sure," said Amy, "that's a fine idea."

Mr. Brothers practised standing up and walking a little. Amy helped him to stand on a rock and Kiko led Sancho beside it. Mr. Brothers stepped on. "This will be better," he sighed, his feet almost dragging on the ground.

Kiko climbed up to the funny-looking saddle, let Amy use the stirrup to climb up and sit behind him.

Rojo had never been ridden double before. The slight weight of Amy behind the saddle caused as much commotion as if a mountain lion had pounced on him. Rojo's head went down toward his ankles. His hind feet kicked up a cloud of dust. Dust and hoofs went skyward

105

as both children spilled over his head.

Sitting on the ground, Kiko said a very naughty word. Amy scrambled up and caught Rojo. It hurt Mr. Brothers' head to laugh as much as he would have liked.

"I'll walk," Amy said firmly.

"We'll take turns riding Rojo. One of us ought to walk beside Mr. Brothers, he might get dizzy."

"I hope you both hurt like the dickens," Mr. Brothers said happily.

Very slowly they proceeded down the brushy trail and through the wire gate. Kiko began worrying about Mia, tied up there on the mountain. "It's too hot for one of us to walk today and my leg hurts some from being thrown. I'll wait here. Amy, you ride Rojo on home with Mr. Brothers, then come back for me on Sancho."

Amy hesitated. "You aren't afraid to ride my horse, are you?" Mr. Brothers asked and Amy couldn't admit her uneasiness.

"Of course not," she said, climbing on.

As it turned out, she handled Rojo very well. They proceeded slowly and she enjoyed the feel of a good horse.

Mr. Brothers went away the next day. He wanted to get new glasses and he wanted to take his aching head to a doctor. He planned never to come back.

15

Very early in the morning, or late in the day when shadows were climbing the hills, were the best times to go to Mia and Tesoro. Now the middle of nearly every day was hot and still and birds made small plaintive sounds. Sometimes Amy could take her lunch and be gone all day long, which was the best way, but this was not always possible.

During the hot hours the mare and colt were sleepy. It was siesta time for all creatures. The corral was shaded at one end by a great live oak and in its shade the children dreamed. Usually both animals stayed under the tree, but sometimes little Tesoro would stretch flat under the hot sun and go to sleep. He would breathe very hard

107

and become wet with sweat.

The children wove wonderful daydreams dealing with a brilliant future for Tesoro and Mia, though how to make reality out of dreams they did not know. They had made a first dream come true, the dream of a little colt growing up protected in a wild place.

Beyond the present situation they could not see, except that things were bound to become difficult. When they had to go to school again, and days became shorter, when winter rains and snows came, then how would they manage to take care of their mare and colt?

"We have a tiger by the tail," Amy remarked one lazy afternoon.

"What's that mean?" asked Kiko.

"Well, if you had a tiger by the tail you couldn't let go. He'd turn around and bite you, maybe eat you up."

"Yes?"

"Well, that's like we have Mia and Tesoro here. Where can we ever move them to that would be near home and still safe? How can we keep them here forever and how can we not?"

Kiko said he didn't know. He stood up and walked to the spring for a drink. The spring did not produce as much water as it had earlier; the pool had shrunk but still it watered the mare and colt and Sancho, as well as all the deer and coyotes and birds and everything else that needed it.

Now he went to the hay cave which was also the tack room and got out Mia's hackamore. "It's starting to cool off and I want to rein her around a little."

He rode Mia at a gallop now and Amy loved to watch Mia's action, the way her black mane rippled. She turned as nimbly as a cow horse, this way and that. Kiko didn't know whether to be more

108

proud of his horse-training ability or more proud of the way Mia had responded; he felt good about both. Tesoro scampered after his mother. Sometimes he felt a sudden burst of excitement and sprinted, his short tail flagged straight up. On days when he wasn't too sleepy Sancho galloped along behind them.

"Now you take her around once," Kiko offered, "and then we'll stop."

To gallop on Mia was as good as floating through the air. She had a wonderful long stride, with just enough motion to make it fun. Amy had learned to ride easily, by balance, not gripping hard with her knees but letting her legs swing free. Her braids bounced, Mia's mane flicked back, and it was all such fun that she circled the clearing three times before Kiko made her stop.

"If we ever let her run too fast or go too long it might not be good for her legs. They let some age get onto these hunters before they run them hard or jump them much. She's not even full-grown yet. But sometime I'm going to try her on a low jump, just to see."

"She's worth a fortune, Kiko. We've got to make her and Tesoro be really ours. How can we get money? Do you suppose if we had lots of money and gave it to Mr. Richie he'd let us have them?"

"I don't know."

"Kiko, I've been thinking. There's more to it than keeping Mia and Tesoro hidden here or anywhere else. They've *got* to be really and truly ours. How can they be?"

Kiko shrugged.

"If we had lots of money," Amy repeated, "and if we pretended that we just found Mia and Tesoro, and then we gave the money to my father and got him to go and talk to Mr. Richie? How mad would

Mr. Richie be? I know what! We wouldn't let him even see the colt—just Mia. After all, he doesn't know what the colt looks like; he could think that the colt died. He couldn't know anything for sure about Tesoro. Somehow I think that loads of money would fix everything."

Kiko snorted. "Where'd *we* ever get any money?"

"I don't know. We'll have to think. But if we could—I wonder if the hermit ever really hid any money around here? Remember, that's what I told Mr. Brothers."

"Well, let's look," said Kiko.

They had no implement for digging, but they delved around in the tumble of broken adobe bricks where the hermit had had his house. They found a broken knife, some rusted tin cans containing nothing but dirt, and a few bits of broken dishes. Kiko salvaged the knife. Though half its blade was broken off, the stubby end that was left was strong enough for slight digging in the hard earth.

"I wonder," mused Amy. "If he buried some money, where would he bury it?"

Kiko looked around—at the rocks on the mountain, at the oaks that grew where they could, at the forest of brush that stretched westward. "I guess he'd put it by something different."

"Something different?"

"Like a specially funny-shaped rock. Or a tree more bent or different some way. Maybe near the spring or in a cave. So's he could remember where it was."

Amy looked long at the mountain. "There's a rock, not too far away. See, Kiko, it is tall and thin and stands straight up like a little tower."

"Maybe we can find a way to go there."

110

Among the boulders the brush grew not tall, having no place for deep roots. Kiko found a narrow trail made by the deer and they followed it toward the stone pinnacle. Where the deer trails started off in the wrong direction they found open ways through sparse brush, and they climbed over rocks. Kiko moved cautiously because all his life he had been aware that rattlesnakes live in such places. He was like a horse that is accustomed to graze in a wild pasture; he was ready to shy.

They reached the tall stone spire, found sagebrush and greasewood thick by its base. There was nowhere to dig. They viewed the problem from all sides, wondered how long it had taken the brush to grow there in case once it had been cleared away and a treasure buried. They were high enough so that they could look down on the corral and the three animals. "From there, which way would he go to hide something?" Amy wondered as she looked about her.

While Kiko started off on another deer trail Amy pushed her way between clumps of chaparral, found clearings between boulders, and then saw a big boulder with an opening in it.

She peered in. It was a natural rock cave, big enough for four or five people to sit in. It had a little overhang, like eaves, to shelter it. "Kiko, come look!" she called.

"Did you find some money?"

"I think I found someone's house."

Kiko hurried back, viewed the opening, picked up small stones and began throwing them inside.

"What for?" Amy asked.

"If there's snakes it will make them rattle. I don't want to go crawling onto a snake."

111

The stones made some lizards scurry for their lives, but no snake hissed or rattled. Kiko waited to make sure, then they crept in. It was not dark, for the opening was large. "Look at all the empty snail shells," Amy said, picking one up to look at its pretty swirled design.

But Kiko was looking for something else. Gently he moved the soft surface of the earth with his hand, brushing dust out of the way. "Hah," he said, and picked up something brown.

"What's that?"

"A piece of pottery, that's what. Look for more."

"Pottery?"

"Broken ollas and stuff. We found an Indian cave. I think there'll be arrowheads, too. Keep looking."

Amy, searching diligently, found more pieces. Soon they had a little stack of pottery shards.

"Somewhere on this mountain there must be some whole ollas hidden in the rocks. You know," said Kiko, his eyes shining, "my father says they're worth money now."

"How much?"

"I don't know, but maybe a lot. I bet we can find a whole olla, not all broken."

"Would that be as good as finding the hermit's money?"

"Maybe."

"Let's look and look."

Kiko was scuffing in the dirt. "Here's an arrowhead. Lookee."

It was made of white quartz, carefully designed and pretty as a jewel. "A good sharp one," Kiko exulted.

Amy gasped. "Here's a tiny blue bead."

"And a shell from the seashore—"

Who could guess that the old stony mountain hid so many wonderful things?

Amy turned to Kiko, her eyes shining. "This is the most wonderful mountain that ever was!"

She had a feeling too deep for words. Somehow this mountain that hid the mare and colt so well was going to take care of everything. Somewhere on this mountain was the answer, if only they could find it.

She looked down at the corral at the black colt who stood with raised head beside his mother. "He's so beautiful," she said, as she had said so many times before. "A little black horse on Black Horse Mountain. Kiko, I bet the wild black stallion used to come up here and look around. I can truly see him when I look at Tesoro. I know he couldn't have been any more beautiful than our colt. Our colt," Amy repeated, "Oh, Kiko, there's times when I know everything's going to turn out all right."

16

FRANK KEPT THINKING to himself, "That Kiko, he is up to something."

Frank didn't know exactly why he felt this way. Kiko was not behaving strangely except that perhaps he was a little better than usual about keeping the woodbox full and washing the dishes. Then away he went, he and the burro and the little girl.

As Frank recalled, Kiko usually was off with his burro most of the days of any vacation. So this was not strange. Ordinarily, however, it had been Kiko's pleasure, when Frank rode the near pastures, to accompany him on Sancho. Kiko had seemed proud to ride with

114

his father, to point out, "That cow has a bad eye; must have got a fox-tail in it, or maybe it's pink-eye."

But not once this summer had Kiko ridden with him. However, in no other summer had Kiko had another child to play with. Probably that was it.

"Anyway," Frank thought, "I got to have a talk with him."

When Kiko had been a small boy, after his mother had died, he had lived on the reservation with his aunt and uncle and cousins. He was only two years old then, and Frank couldn't possibly look after him and tend to his job too. He saw him often and loved him very much and was glad when at last Kiko was old enough to go to school, old enough to look after himself after school, and the two could live together.

It was then that Frank got Kiko a burro so that the child could learn about animals and hills and never be lonely. Frank himself had had a burro named Sancho when he was a little boy in Old Mexico and he knew what good friends a boy and a burro can be.

One evening, as father and son sat eating their beans and hamburger, Frank asked, "What do you do all day, anyway?"

Kiko swallowed a mouthful of beans. "Oh, we ride around and pretend different things."

"Like what?"

"Like being Indian scouts. We look for arrowheads, too, and ollas. Would we get a lot of money if we found an olla?"

"What do you want money for?"

Kiko shrugged. "It's good to have. Maybe we could buy a horse."

"So now you want a horse. The burro not good enough?"

"Sancho's very good. I mean we want a mare, too. Then I could ride her and Amy could ride Sancho."

"You want to buy a mare?"

"I like mares. Maybe someday raise a colt."

Frank looked thoughtful. "Too bad you couldn't have got that mare, Mia."

Kiko looked uneasy. "Do you think she is far away?"

"Who knows?"

"Who knows?" Kiko echoed.

"Kiko, my son, you wouldn't lie to me ever, would you?"

"What you mean, Papa?"

"Just what I say. You would never lie to me about anything?"

"I would never want to lie to you, Papa."

"That is good. This man, Señor Brothers, he asked me about you and the little girl, Amy."

"Asked about us?"

"He said, did I know where you went all the time, did you have a secret?"

"He did?" Kiko tried to make his face express great surprise.

"Yes. What do you know about this?"

"Well, Papa, we were with him most of the time."

"Yes. But I think—I do not know—but by golly, that fellow he believed maybe you kids knew something."

"Knew something?" Again Kiko seemed astonished.

"About that mare."

"Oh, Papa," Kiko cried. "I hope no mean man gets them."

"I hope so too."

Kiko didn't care for this conversation. He sighed and looked at his father helplessly.

116

"Kiko, it is just that I wish for you to be a good boy, and I guess, by golly, in summer it is all right for you to enjoy vacation because when school starts you are busy all the time. But you must think about what kind of man you are going to be one day. What you think, Kiko?"

"Like you," said Kiko. "I want to know everything about cows and horses. I want to know how to drive a truck and how to buck bales of hay. And how to drive a tractor and disc and plant and harrow, and drive a mowing machine and know how to rake, and drive a hay baler. Like you can do everything. Shoe horses. Ride and rope. Break horses. What do you think, Papa?"

"I think yes. A man, when he can do all those things good, he's never out of a job. Maybe you'll have a little bunch of cows of your own someday."

Kiko nodded happily. "A bunch of cows. And a mare. And wouldn't it be fine if, maybe, someday the mare had a little colt. And he would grow into a fine black horse, like the old wild stallion that lived in the canyon and ran on Black Horse Mountain—"

"That would be a fine thing to have, Kiko. When you grow up to be a good man, and you work hard, you'll have these things."

Kiko thought, "Papa doesn't know how hard I work already."

He looked out through the open door. There was daylight left and Kiko squirmed uneasily, thinking that when the light grew dimmer he wanted to sneak two more sacks of hay out of the barn. He hoped Frank wouldn't want to keep on talking. He hated deceiving him. He'd tried his best to get around his questions without actually telling a lie; but his conscience hurt him. Ordinarily, he found it pleasant to sit like a man, talking to the man who was his father.

117

17

THEY SAT IN the dry grass of the clearing and each held an animal at the end of a long rope. Amy had the colt and Kiko had the mare. Sancho was free to wander about, but he had eaten his fill and stood dozing in the shade. While he slept his ears drooped and his lower lip hung down; one hip sagged. His tail stayed awake to switch flies and occasionally his ears revived and waved around. The annoyance of flies was part of his summer life and he protested stolidly and methodically and mechanically.

The day was warm and had turned sultry. No one had the energy to explore the mountain. Large thunderheads had risen up in the

118

east, shining white with tints of blue in their folds. They looked cold as ice cream. Beyond the eastern mountains the hot desert air had made the clouds climb up.

It had seemed a good time to teach Mia and Tesoro about grazing on long ropes. The first thing each did was to turn around and cause the ropes to tighten around all their feet. Kiko let them struggle until it seemed as if they were in danger of receiving rope burns; then the ropes were slackened a little. Now both animals were learning to step over and to turn without getting quite so badly tangled.

Tesoro got one hind hoof completely wrapped around, felt panicked and would have done damage to himself if he had been tied to some solid thing. As it was, Amy let him have more slack and finally he was able to get himself worked free.

It would take a great deal of practice before mare or colt could be as well stake-broken as Sancho. Sancho could be tethered to graze anywhere at all and was clever enough not to wind his rope around even the smallest bush that happened to be in the way. He knew exactly how to step and turn without getting tangled.

The children felt too languid to do much talking. This particular teaching chore was just right for this day. Dreamily, they watched the clouds billow and form into pictures of creatures and fairy castles. A cloud even ventured in front of the sun and a lovely cool shadow dropped over the hills, seeming to wander along like a stray grazing animal.

Suddenly there was a rumble. Mia and Tesoro were startled, Amy jumped, Kiko stood up. "By golly, thunder. Maybe we'll get a summer rain."

119

Lightning flashed sharply, making a stab at the clouds. Thunder rolled and Kiko cried, "Hold tight to the colt!"

Tesoro was wild-eyed, all for trying to run to escape whatever it was the sky was trying to throw at him. Mia snorted, then whinnied to him, and he pressed close to her side.

Slow, fat drops of warm rain began to fall and there was the exciting fragrance of rain touching the sun-baked earth, of drops falling on dry grass and dusty leaves. For an instant, everything was bright in one dart of lightning. Thunder boomed. Sancho took to his heels, Mia and Tesoro wanted to run, but were anchored to the children and couldn't drag them more than a few feet. As if the lightning had torn the clouds apart, the rain fell more and more swiftly, slicing hills and mountains completely out of sight.

Tesoro, no longer filled with bravado, became a young frightened foal. He crowded tight against Mia, who stood with her rump to the storm and her head low. There was no more banging of thunder, only the wild sound of torrents of rain.

Animals and children were soaked and dripping, but this rain was warm, and certainly doing a good job of washing everything. Mud puddles began spreading into ponds, tiny trickles grew as they traveled down the mountain, small rivulets went surging toward low places, some of them carving new waterways with the fierceness of their hurry. Everything about this rain was so sudden and dramatic it was easy to believe that really a cloud had burst.

The children could have run to shelter in the hay cave—there would even have been room for mare and colt to poke their heads in—but it was too much fun receiving this shower bath straight from the sky. Tesoro's mane and tail became more kinky than ever. He

120

was as black and shining as a patent-leather slipper, while his mother's bay coat was polished to a coppery brightness.

After a few minutes the rain ceased to pound so hard. Soon there were only a few hesitant drops and a ray of intense sunlight flashed down through a cloud-hole, making wet boulders look like melting gold, making trees and hills light up so vividly it seemed as if they themselves were producing the light.

Everywhere were sounds of dripping, splashing and flowing. The mountain was singing with all its new water courses. A great bright rainbow arched from somewhere on their mountain across deep cuts of canyons to mountains toward Mexico. It was so bright that one of it was not enough; there was a reflection so that the children stared at a great double rainbow.

"*Arco celeste*," said Kiko in wonderment. "Never have I seen so bold a one."

Very slowly the colors melted back into the sky and disappeared. Amy and Kiko turned their attention to immediate surroundings, amazed at how changed their familiar place had become now that it was all shining and noisy with rain rivers. Steam rose from the warm wet earth, making clouds along the ground, and everyone's legs disappeared which seemed remarkably odd. Sancho, who had found comfort behind a big boulder, came walking to them on what seemed to be no legs at all. The animals' coats steamed, steam rose from the children's soaked jeans. But no one was cold. Finally the little earth fog wandered away, mists and cloud wisps played for awhile around every hill and canyon, until the sun came out in earnest.

Kiko went to see how wet the hay might have got, planning to spread it out in the sun if need be. But the barn of boulders had sheltered everything well. He picked up Mia's hackamore. "Let's ride around and look at all the rivers."

Amy adjusted a rope loop around Sancho's nose and scrambled up onto his wet back. Tesoro went flashing around, running in circles, flagging up his tail. Kiko, proudly riding Mia, led off.

They hadn't gone far before they came to a small roaring waterway that had cut a ditch into the earth. Mia stopped suddenly, stared at the brown water and snorted. She could have stepped across easily, but she acted as if she thought she might get her hoofs dangerously wet and she tried to turn back.

"Oh, come on," Kiko said, urging her forward, tapping her sides with his heels.

It was as if Mia unfurled invisible wings. From a standstill she lifted herself much higher than need be, leaped much wider than need be, and landed on light feet. This delighted her so much that she gave an extra buck-jump and nearly spilled Kiko. He recovered control, galloped her to the next stream, and she flew over that. Tesoro put on speed to catch up, cleared the first ditch easily, but went splashing into the second, jumping not quite far enough. It was wider than the first and he had misjudged. However, he thought it all fun and leaped out to send his heels skyward, then propelled himself faster.

Kiko brought Mia to a stop and turned to watch Sancho who stepped calmly over the first stream and waded across the second.

"Oh," said Amy, "I wish Sancho had jumped. That would have been fun!"

Kiko obligingly slid off and found a mounting block for Amy.

"Try it. It's easy, but hang on to her mane if you're afraid."

Amy felt glad to have Mia's black mane for, as she galloped toward the water, her stomach did a funny thing, as if she were in a fast-moving elevator. When Mia suddenly took to the air, Amy's heart gave an extra throb. Mia skimmed to earth, Amy shot forward, then regained herself, Mia's long legs took her to the second jump—then up and over.

It could have been only a second or two that Amy and Mia were airborne, but it was the most gloriously happy interval of time Amy had ever experienced.

Little Tesoro was in the spirit of the thing and wanted to do nothing but run around and leap streams. Sancho, never one to overdo anything, sighed sadly.

"By golly," said Kiko, "these two sure like to jump."

18

Early on Saturday morning, a few days later, when Kiko and Sancho stopped at Amy's house, Kiko said, "Today before we go to the mare and colt, we go to the reservation to visit my cousins."

"Why?" asked Amy, scrambling up behind Kiko.

"There is something to see," Kiko answered. "My aunt came last night and she told us. You know that day it rained so much? Well, my cousin's dog was barking, and they went to look, and in a lot of water coming right down the hill behind their house was a tiny fawn, all half-drowned and cold and hungry. So they have him. He thinks he is a little goat now because their mother goat likes him

124

and feeds him with her kid. I think he will live."

"I never heard of such a thing," said Amy.

"Neither did my father. He says it is kind of late for fawns, most are born earlier. This little fawn really was lost, but my father says that if I find one hiding somewhere I must never touch it. Their mothers hide them and go back to them, and if people touch them their mother doesn't like the smell, maybe doesn't like the fawn any more."

"I wish the deer knew we wouldn't hurt their fawns."

"The wild animals think all people are bad. They have to be scared of us because they can't tell who isn't going to hurt them. My father says that a long time ago, at the beginning, animals weren't scared of us, but we got mean."

"Your father knows lots of things."

Kiko nodded.

"He wouldn't be mean to children or animals?"

"I don't think he'd want to be."

"I wonder how mad he'd be if ever he found out about Mia and Tesoro?"

Kiko shrugged. "Plenty mad, I guess, on account of how he has to work for Mr. Richie and Mr. Richie might even fire him or something. He might think my father stole Mia."

"I was only wondering, if maybe we told your father all about everything, what he'd do."

"Oh, golly," said Kiko. "I'd be too scared! How about your folks?"

"I don't know. They seem pretty good about letting me do things, especially after we moved here. But you never can tell."

125

They considered the adult world and how unpredictable it was.

"Your aunt and uncle," Amy said. "They like the little fawn?"

"Oh yes, my aunt likes it very much. They both do," Kiko answered, sliding off to open the reservation gate. "My aunt likes any kind of babies."

Amy thought of something else. "Maybe we'll see Tesoro's father. What's his name?"

"They named him Comanche. That's some Indian tribe somewhere."

"This is where Mia ran to that spring?"

"And jumped this gate, I guess."

"And now we have Tesoro."

They thought what a strange and wonderful thing it was that Tesoro had chanced to come into being.

They rode past a few little houses. Dogs barked at them and small, solemn children stared. The road twisted its way into a canyon, and there were Kiko's cousins, a girl and two boys, playing with a fawn in the dooryard.

The little creature had great deep eyes, ears like pointed flower petals, a dark nose. Loveliest of all were its narrow legs, ending with the tiniest of shining black cloven hoofs. Amy looked at a pattern of white spots in a soft brown coat and began to realize that at last she was seeing a really-truly small fawn. She slid off Sancho and hurried to touch it.

By now it felt sure of its place in the world. It was unafraid of the children and their dog, it was fond of the mother goat and her little white kid. Compared with the fawn, the pretty little goat baby looked coarse and clumsy. Both little animals had short perky tails.

126

"Golly," said Kiko, staring delightedly. "What's his name?"

"We've been calling him Bucky," the girl answered.

Kid and fawn wandered happily from one child to another while the mother goat, tethered to a tree, observed that all was well. The dog, which Amy noticed hopped on three legs, from time to time licked the fawn's face.

Amy knew the children because they had been fellow passengers on the school bus. The boys were twins and their names were Kennie and Rudie. The girl, Anatasia, who wore her straight black hair cut to just below her ears with an even, shining line of bangs across her forehead, was Amy's size and twelve years old. The twins were two years younger.

Amy asked, "What happened to the dog?"

"He lost his foot in a coyote trap. A long while ago. Poor Cisco."

Hopping about with one front paw missing, Cisco, black and white and lop-eared, seemed to find life no problem. He was happy with his children and animal friends.

When kid and fawn grew hungry the fawn made an odd little mewing sound, not the kind of sound you would expect a fawn to make. Amy had imagined that a fawn would bleat like a kid or a lamb. Instead it mewed, and it and the kid raced to the mother goat.

One on each side, they bunted and nursed vigorously while the nannie turned her head to touch first one, then the other. The up-turned tails twitched enthusiastically and all the children laughed. Filled with milk, the baby animals grew sleepy and settled down together in the shade.

"Where's Comanche?" Amy asked.

"I guess he's up on the hill behind the house," Anatasia answered, and stood up to look. "There, under that oak."

The brown horse stood dozing, switching flies. "He's a good horse," said Anatasia. "He doesn't care if all three of us ride him at once."

"Do you like horses?" Amy wanted to know.

"Oh yes."

"Do you ride around lots of places?"

"When it isn't too hot."

"We got to go now," said Kiko, thinking about Mia and Tesoro.

"Where does this road go?" Amy asked him.

"Oh, on up the canyon, past some houses, and then up the mountain a ways. It just ends."

"No trail goes on?"

"Mostly just brush."

"Couldn't we get through?"

Kiko glanced at his cousins. Anatasia's big black eyes were filled with curiosity.

"Keep quiet," Kiko hissed.

But Amy was thinking that here were ones who would share their feeling about the mare and colt; these were of their world as opposed to the adult world. She was considering the days ahead when they would all be in school for long hours, when afternoons would become short, when the many trips down the canyon and up the mountainside would be difficult.

"Kiko," she whispered. "Let's tell them."

He shook his head firmly. "Come on," he commanded. "Let's go."

Anatasia thought, "Those kids are up to something."

128

Obviously, they had some sort of secret and she didn't like being left out of it. After all, she was Kiko's very own cousin, and if she didn't go to his home to play it wasn't her fault; it was that Mr. Richie didn't want Indian kids around. Ordinarily, it made little difference to her whether she went to Kiko's or not. She saw him from time to time anyway and she had plenty of children and animals to play with on the reservation.

But now he had this new friend, this blue-eyed one, and whatever it was Kiko was up to, this girl was mixed up in it. They were together all the time. At least they were wandering about somewhere whenever the girl's mother didn't make her stay home. And this Amy, she wasn't even a California child, she hadn't ever been on a ranch before she came here. She'd probably never in all her life ridden a good horse. It was a wonder she didn't fall off the burro, Anatasia thought, unaccountably feeling scornful toward Amy. Suddenly it annoyed her very much that Kiko was leaving his very own cousins out of some private secret and sharing it with an outsider.

At first it hadn't seemed important, but the more she pondered about it the more her displeasure grew. It was frustrating because she couldn't possibly imagine what Kiko and Amy were up to. "Probably nothing," she told herself. "Just something they're playing. Maybe they have a secret tree house, or maybe they found a cave. Rudie and Kennie and I ought to have a secret and not let them in on it. Something real good. But what?"

She could think of nothing. Anyway, she had an idea that Kiko wouldn't care even if they did taunt him with their secret, whatever it could be. Kiko had a firm way of going about his own affairs and not caring what other people did. He was a difficult boy to annoy.

129

If they couldn't manage to bother him with their secret, then there was no use having one.

She spoke to her brothers. "Kiko has some secret, him and that girl. They won't tell us."

Rudie looked surprised. "I didn't know."

Kennie said, "What makes you think so?"

"You're stupid," Anatasia told them, feeling cross at everybody.

"Well, they didn't *say* they had a secret."

"You could tell, if you had any sense."

"How?"

"Oh, the way they act. They were whispering. And where do they go all the time? I don't think Kiko ever stays home."

"He never did anyway. He's always going on the burro."

"Maybe they think they found a gold mine or something."

"I think they look for arrowheads and ollas and things."

Anatasia sighed. "I think it's something big and important. They're up to something, Kiko and that city girl!"

"She's nice."

Kennie added, "Funny blue eyes. You don't see too many that color around here."

"They're on *her* side," Anatasia thought bitterly. She refused to speak further and her brothers didn't know why she was so annoyed.

She promised herself, "I'll find out what their silly secret is."

Anatasia was fairly sure that on a Monday Mr. Richie wouldn't be on the ranch. Sometimes he came in the middle of the week, often he came on weekends. She thought that in the city he went to some kind of office where he counted his money all day, and

Anatasia had an idea that Monday was always office day.

Monday morning was a busy time for Anatasia, too. She had to help her mother do the family washing. This was done in a washing machine that was operated by a noisy gasoline engine, a thing which sputtered and coughed and broke down frequently. But they had to use it, or do vast washings by hand, because there was no electricity on the reservation. Rudie and Kennie had to be on hand on Monday mornings because only they could coax the machine into working.

Ordinarily it didn't matter if the washing took all day. The washing machine stood outside under a big shady oak, and, if Rudie and Kennie would help, it was not too much work to carry buckets of water from the spring behind the house. In winter their mother built a fire outdoors and heated all the water; that saved one's hands from becoming numb. In summer they didn't bother to heat the water and the clothes got just as clean. It was pleasant splashing around in the cool soapy water, rinsing the clothes in fresh clear water after they went through the wringer. The machine wouldn't operate the wringer; it had a handle that had to be turned and, if the twins would cooperate, the children took turns.

Washing the clothes was woman's work and Anatasia's mother never insisted that the boys help, except that they had to deal with the engine when it ceased to operate. That was man's work. The actual hauling of the water, handling the clothes, turning the wringer and putting the clothes on the line were tasks the boys did not have to do unless they volunteered. Since they had to stay home anyway to keep the machine going, they were not above giving their mother and sister a hand with the rest of the work. If they had plans for something special they wanted to do that day, the twins would work

131

to hurry up the job.

This Monday morning, as Anatasia went to the spring with her water buckets, she heard the boys attempting to start the machine and wondered if she should tell them what she planned to do today. It might make them help more and get the work over with sooner. On the other hand, she was still peeved at them and when she thought further she decided that she'd do better alone anyway. She planned to be sneaky and furtive, and that was a thing better done by one's self.

As it turned out, the boys didn't help at all. They sensed Anatasia's antagonism toward them and they would cooperate about nothing. It even seemed to take them extra-long to coax the machine into working each time it gave out.

Anatasia worked as hard and as fast as she could, but it was noon before the last pair of jeans and the last sock were hung on the line. Then it was time to help her mother get lunch.

As they were finishing the meal, Anatasia said, "Mama, can I go riding on Comanche this afternoon? I did all the helping with the wash and the boys would hardly do anything."

"Aw—" the twins started to protest.

"You are lazy good-for-nothings," Anatasia told them. "May I, Mama?"

"Where do you want to go?"

"Oh, just around. It's not too hot today, there's a cool breeze. I just want to take a little ride on the horse. Tomorrow I'll help iron."

"I guess that's all right. Don't you want the boys to go?"

"I'm tired of them. I just want to be alone. Besides, it's no fun with

132

three of us and only one horse. I ought to have Comanche because I am the oldest and Papa could get a burro for the twins."

The twins looked at her with fury.

"Don't start a fight now," their mother said wearily. "Why don't you boys go find the horse for your sister?"

But they wouldn't, and Anatasia had to hunt all over the pasture before she found Comanche dozing under an oak.

She decided, as she rode onto Mr. Richie's land, that if she saw any of the men and they asked what she was doing here, she'd say she was hunting for a stray cow. It was possible that one of the Indian cows could get through a fence and onto Mr. Richie's land. If so, Anatasia had a perfect right to ride looking for it. The men wouldn't care anyway. It was only Mr. Richie who was silly and fussy, and he wouldn't be here.

She rode straight to Amy's house. It was a fine big white stucco house that had been on the place when Mr. Richie bought it, only, swell as it was, it wasn't swell enough and he had built a better one for himself and his family.

His children were big kids now who went to college and seldom came to the ranch, even in vacation. Anatasia thought they should like to come, especially since there was a big, beautiful swimming pool by the house. She herself would dearly love to have a house with a swimming pool beside it. Most of the time the big house was vacant, and once a week the wife of one of the ranch hands came and cleaned it. Anatasia wondered why it needed cleaning when it so seldom had anyone in it.

Amy's house, with its red-tiled roof, also looked like the kind of house rich people lived in, and Anatasia felt slightly timid as she

133

tied Comanche to the garden fence, went through a gate and along a path between flowers, up to the front porch. The porch had a smooth red cement floor which Anatasia admired. She looked through a screen door into what she considered an expensive-looking room and knocked not very loudly. The lady who came to the door was Amy's mother all right. She had yellow hair and blue eyes like Amy.

She looked friendly and smiled as Anatasia asked, "Is Amy here, please?"

"No, she isn't. She and Kiko took their lunches and went off with the burro. They should be home after awhile. Are you Kiko's cousin? The little girl who has the pet fawn? Amy told us about going to your house and seeing the little fawn."

"Yes, ma'am, I'm Anatasia. I thought I would come play with Kiko and Amy today. I'm tired of playing with my brothers."

The lady laughed. "Brothers can be bores sometimes."

"Mine are extra awful. They're twins."

"Yes, I suppose that would make it twice as bad. Doesn't your mother worry when you're out riding around by yourself?"

"No, ma'am. Only she likes it better when we all go. Or at least if there's two of us together. But it really doesn't matter. What could hurt us?"

"Snakes?" conjectured Amy's mother.

"Only rattlesnakes are bad. And we always remember to be careful."

"I suppose so. Amy wants to be riding that burro all the time. But sometimes I worry a little and I do try to make her stay home once in awhile. But I really believe it's good for her to be enjoying

134

this freedom."

"Yes, ma'am. But I wonder—I don't suppose you know where they go all the time?"

"Well—down the canyon, I think. Amy is always talking about what fun it is to play down there by the spring where it's shady. I'll have to walk down and see it some evening when it's cool. I haven't learned how to ride a horse."

"Oh, that's easy," said Anatasia, surprised that anyone had to learn to do so natural a thing. "But my mother doesn't ride horses either, only that's because she's so fat. You don't look very heavy; I bet you could ride. Only you couldn't wear that pretty dress, you'd need jeans."

Amy's mother looked at Comanche standing quietly by the fence. "Don't you use a saddle?"

"We haven't any. My dad has one but he won't let us kids use it. Anyway, I like to ride bareback."

"How ever do you get on?"

"Oh, it's easy. I'll show you. I have to go now, anyway. I want to find Amy and Kiko."

Anatasia gave a little leap, swung her right leg over Comanche's back. It was as if she had floated up, Amy's mother thought, watching with admiration as she rode off.

Suddenly Anatasia thought, "Oh my, I shouldn't have told that lady I was looking for those kids. I don't want them to know I'm trailing them." She turned and rode back.

"Ma'am?" she called. Amy's mother still stood by the door. She was thinking how beautiful this child looked, riding so proudly. Anatasia's brown skin showed through torn spots in her shirt, her jeans were old and faded, she wore no shoes. Yet she looked like a princess on the little brown horse.

"I guess you think this is funny. But please don't tell Amy and Kiko I was out looking for them," Anatasia continued, a little breathlessly."Because I have to go home pretty soon and maybe I won't have time to ride all the way and find them. I just wanted to surprise them, that's all. If I do find them that's okay, but if I don't Kiko will laugh at me for not being able to follow the old burro's tracks. I'll play with them some other day and that will be all right. So please don't say anything. I'm not supposed to be over on this ranch anyway. I ought to go home pretty quick."

The lady didn't look surprised. She must have known that sometimes children liked to be secretive. "That's all right," she agreed. "I won't tell them. But you'll come back another time, won't you?'

"Yes, ma'am, I will. Thank you." And Anatasia rode off, thinking how much she liked this lady who, when she was a little girl, must have looked exactly as Amy looked now.

19

It DIDN'T TAKE Anatasia long to pick up the small u-shaped tracks of Sancho, plain on the dusty trail. When she reached Black Horse Spring she saw the tracks of Amy's tennis shoes and the barefoot tracks of Kiko. They had stopped for a drink and perhaps to rest a little. She let Comanche drink and then she took a few swallows of good cold water.

Before she started on, she tied Comanche off the trail in the chaparral, broke a piece of brush and dusted out her tracks and his. She proceeded, keeping off the main trail, winding through the brush, returning from time to time to check the trail again. This was puzzling for, beyond the spring, the tracks disappeared for long stretches.

When she reached the place where the canyon turned and twisted off to the left, she could find no more tracks at all. She back-tracked and lost the trail again. Then she rode the other way and this brought her to the ordinary wire gate, beyond which was the mountain part of reservation land. There were no burro tracks here, no sign that anyone had used this gate regularly. The tall brown grass stood upright on both sides of the gate.

As she sat there on Comanche, puzzling and pondering, he lifted his head and pricked up his ears as if, straight ahead in the brush beyond the gate, he had heard something. As Anatasia held still, listening, she heard something too. It was the voice of Amy talking to Kiko and the sound was coming nearer.

Anatasia turned Comanche and galloped back up the canyon. She rode up the canyon side, hid in a thicket of scrub oak. From here she could look down on them as they rode by. They were not likely to look up and see her, unless Comanche whinnied.

She remembered reading somewhere that when Indians didn't want a horse to whinny they tied a stone on his tail. A horse, just as he is about to whinny, lifts his tail a little and so a weight hung on it would, presumably, puzzle him into quietness. However, this didn't seem to be a very easy or practical thing to do. Anatasia decided it would be better to slide off, stand by Comanche's head and grab his nose if he seemed ready to whinny.

She waited. After awhile she heard Amy again. Kiko wasn't saying a word, just riding stolidly along. Anatasia couldn't hear what Amy was talking about as Sancho came into sight, trudging patiently, nodding his head as he walked. With ears at attention, Comanche peered down at them while Anatasia cupped his muzzle in her two hands.

She held still for some minutes after they had disappeared. She didn't get back on Comanche. She walked instead, leading him down the hill. Walking, studying the earth closely and proceeding very slowly, she tried to make sure not to lose any tracks again.

It was difficult to follow where Sancho had left the trail and walked on dry grass and wound through brush. Obviously, Kiko had chosen devious ways in order to leave no trail. No one would be likely to notice the burro's tracks unless he had a reason for tracking him—and was as determined as Anatasia. Several times she had to turn back to where she had last seen tracks and start all over again.

Then it occurred to her that she could abandon the idea of following tracks, for, having heard the children and Sancho coming through the brush on the reservation side of the fence, she knew which direction to go. She had only to find out where they got through the fence without using the gate.

This wasn't difficult. She pushed through the brush and followed the fence until she found where Kiko had cut the wires, made twists of baling wire, and thus constructed a secret gate.

She took down the wires, led Comanche through, put the wires back up. She jumped on Comanche and in a very few minutes she had found the scar of the trail through the tall lilac. When she reached the clearing she and Comanche froze in amazement.

Mia and Tesoro were equally amazed. The black colt stood with his head high and his eyes bugged out—stood so rigidly staring that his muscles quivered. His nostrils twitched. "He-he-he," he squealed

139

to the horse who was his father. Mia touched her colt reassuringly, then focused her attention on horse and rider.

Anatasia felt herself trembling with excitement and her emotions were confused. So *this* was their secret! She could never have guessed it in a million years. Those kids, those little kids, had a stolen mare and a colt hidden here!

She continued to stare helplessly as slowly her mind began sorting things out. This mare was Mia, the one everyone had been looking for. This was the colt that Comanche had sired before they had made a gelding out of him. This most beautiful black colt was the one that Mr. Richie wasn't going to let Mia keep. But somehow those kids had got the mare here where she could foal in secret. Here—unless someone else should turn out to be as smart as Anatasia—they were safe.

Anatasia's next emotion was pure glee and a grand feeling of self-esteem. It made her laugh out loud. Without very much trouble she had accomplished what all those important grownups hadn't been able to do.

She slid off Comanche, tied him to a bush, and walked toward the corral. Tesoro came to her and trustingly put his muzzle into her outstretched hand.

Kiko halted the burro. "You talk too much," he told Amy. "Look."
"At what?"
"The trail. See? Fresh horse tracks."
"One of the cowboys, most likely."
"No. They all ride shod horses. These are barefoot tracks. They come down the canyon as far as the spring, almost. I didn't see any

by the spring. But it looks like somebody tried to follow us."

"But why?"

"To find out something, I guess. Maybe they're looking for Mia again."

Amy was dismayed. "But I thought they'd given up."

Kiko shrugged.

"Could it be just some kids out riding? Someone from the reservation? Perhaps one of your cousins?"

"Naw. They won't ride on Mr. Richie's place."

"Well, you said the tracks didn't go on beyond the spring. So they didn't get very far."

"There might be some down past the place I started looking." Kiko was puzzled. "But where did they go? They come down the canyon and they don't go back."

"Well, maybe whoever it is rode up the canyon side somewhere and on somewhere else. Sure it couldn't be Anatasia or the twins?"

"What would they be doing over here?"

"Looking for us?"

"What'd they do that for?"

"I don't know. Mr. Brothers couldn't be back, could he?"

"He's not back. My father would say something if he was. Anyway, he isn't."

Amy said, "I still think we ought to tell those kids about Mia and Tesoro. They could help. We'd be glad later when school starts."

"No. It's safer without too many knowing. Me, I don't need help anyway. Maybe some days I will not go to school, I will go to the horses."

Amy sighed. Life for Kiko was so simple. It made her feel annoyed with him. "Well, anyway, you can't always do everything. And I know we ought to tell those kids. Maybe I'll tell them anyway."

"You better not," said Kiko so firmly that Amy felt a surge of anger.

"What makes you so bossy anyhow?" she demanded. "You always think you know everything. I guess I have as much right to say what we should do and what we shouldn't."

Kiko shrugged as if her words were too unimportant for further comment.

"I won't even go with you tomorrow if that's how you feel," she said as they neared home. She slid off the burro as he was still walking along, ran across a field and into the house by the back door. Had she gone the other way she might possibly have noticed Comanche's tracks by the front gate.

Amy felt so worried and so annoyed at Kiko that she was almost glad when she remembered that she wasn't going to be allowed to go with Kiko the next day anyway. Her mother had said something about wanting to wash her hair. It might be good for Kiko to think she was so mad she wouldn't go with him. She'd like to stay home until he asked for her help.

But that wouldn't work because, for one thing, she couldn't possibly stay away from Mia and Tesoro very long, and in the second place it wouldn't make a bit of difference to Kiko. He and Sancho would just go poking along, not even noticing that she wasn't with them.

"I can go by myself without Mr. Kiko," she thought. "Tesoro and Mia are as much mine as his."

As Amy had surmised, Kiko didn't appear to notice whether she went with him or not. He didn't even seem to know that she was mad at him.

Kiko had a worrisome problem that should have been Amy's problem too. Someone was interested in his comings and goings, someone was trying to find out about Mia, and it couldn't be Mr. Brothers. Kiko's mind fumbled with one idea and then another and arrived at no conclusion, except that he had better be even more careful than usual. He and Sancho traveled in roundabout ways.

Anyway, no one had found the mare and colt yet; at least Kiko could see no evidence of an intruder in the hermit's clearing. If anyone had been there he had certainly managed to cover up his tracks.

Anatasia was having fun. She too was being exceedingly furtive and roundabout. She could not resist going back whenever she could to look with rapture at the little black horse. Her ankles and bare feet were more scratched than usual from all her travels through the brush to avoid people on the upper part of Mr. Richie's land, to avoid Amy and Kiko in the canyon and on the mountain.

She considered the fact that they seldom seemed to be together any more. She wondered, rather gleefully, if they had had a fight.

When she had first seen Mia and Tesoro she had wondered what she could do with her newly discovered information. She finally decided there was nothing she wanted to do, for certainly she wasn't going to let any adult know where the lost mare was.

The thing that might be fun to do about it would be to worry Kiko and thus pay him back for not letting her into the secret. But that seemed slightly mean because he had been good when, somehow, he and Amy had managed to hide Mia and save her colt.

143

Anyway, it was probable that already Kiko was worried. Careful as she'd been, he must have seen some tracks somewhere. Anatasia wondered why he hadn't guessed that it was she who was on his trail, for he should be able to recognize Comanche's tracks. Perhaps Kiko was assuming that none of the Indian kids dared go poking around on Mr. Richie's land. If that was what he thought, he certainly didn't know his own cousin very well. Anatasia was not one to be easily intimidated. Kiko should know that she wouldn't seek an encounter with Mr. Richie, but she would come on his land if she needed to. And she would know how to avoid being seen by him or anyone.

Amy, meanwhile, whenever opportunity offered, went hurrying down the canyon on her own two feet, wishing all the time that she was riding Sancho. When she and Kiko met at the corral she made a point of noticing him as little as possible. It wasn't a happy arrangement.

Tesoro liked it all because he was seeing more people at more different times. He whinnied whenever he saw Anatasia, who usually brought him an apple or carrot or crust of bread. She found the hay cave and saw the brush and curry-comb and enjoyed applying the dandy-brush until she could almost see her reflection in his polished black coat.

"How beautiful Tesoro's coat looks," Amy thought, and concluded that Kiko had been doing some extra grooming. Kiko thought that Amy must have been using the brush with frequency.

He didn't like Amy to be making these trips on her own. Kiko believed that they should either come together or she should stay home. Amy was one more person to be followed by whoever was interested in their affairs. Amy was doubling the danger and perhaps she wasn't being as careful as she should be.

Finally, worried beyond silence, Kiko spoke of the problem. "Someone follows us sometimes."

"Well, that's what you thought once. You mean someone still is? Like Mr. Brothers did?"

Kiko shrugged. "Guess so."

"Who?"

Kiko shrugged again.

"What'll we do?"

"Watch, I guess. I don't know." This was worse than when Mr. Brothers had been here, for at least they'd known who he was and where he was. All that they knew now was that someone was prowling about who shouldn't be.

Yet Amy felt a sudden gladness. She hadn't enjoyed being mad at Kiko, she had felt lonely and left out. Now they were reunited by a worry—which was not good, but it gave her a feeling of warmth. This was like the beginning, when they had plotted and planned and worried together.

"I know what," she said. "If someone follows you and Sancho, I'll follow them and see who it is."

"How?"

"Well, you and Sancho start off and I'll wait a long time, give whoever it is a chance to get started. Then I'll follow along. We'll have the person between us—you could even turn and ride back, see whoever it is, and then I'd be coming along."

"Then what?"

"Nothing. Only we'd know who it was."

145

"No."

"Why not?"

Kiko thought for a moment. "It would be better, maybe, if we start out together, like always, on Sancho. Then one of us, maybe me, could drop off and hide and watch."

"Yes. And after a long time I could ride back and see who you found. I hope it's nobody really bad, like a horse thief or a cattle rustler."

"If it looked like somebody bad we wouldn't let him see us."

"Maybe we could think of some way to scare him out."

"How?"

"I don't know. We'd think of something. Look what we did to Mr. Brothers. Probably it isn't any criminal, though I'm afraid it's somebody getting suspicious of us and looking for Mia again. I thought they'd given up. I'd really rather have it be someone bad like an escaped prisoner or something."

"Me too."

"Oh, Kiko," Amy exclaimed, feeling happy again. "I'm glad I'm not mad at you any more."

Kiko looked only mildly surprised. "I didn't know you was," he said.

20

Since they had no idea whether they were being followed only on certain days, or every day, or which day it might be, Kiko and Amy found that they had to have enduring patience. Whenever one or the other of them waited in the brush on the canyon side, nobody happened to come along. Time inched slowly. Kiko's problem was that it was his nature to go to sleep whenever he wasn't doing anything very active. Amy's problem was that she grew bored waiting, though she amused herself by watching the birds and ground squirrels and hoping some deer would come walking by.

Anatasia soon became aware of their plans to trap her and she

147

laughed to herself. One day she hid from them, up on the canyon side, while she watched Kiko creep into some brush further down the slope.

In the coolness of an early morning she decided to visit the mare and colt before Kiko and Amy might come. The twins were going with their father to cut wood, their mother was going to visit a lady in town. Anatasia could do what she liked, and to go to the mare and colt was exactly what she liked. She would have time to play with the colt and when she heard Amy and Kiko coming she would get into a brushy spot up on the mountain and enjoy looking down on them.

When she reached the clearing it was still early enough to be cool. Birds should have been singing, but none were. Tesoro didn't whinny. Anatasia stopped and stared. Mia was snorting and watching something in which Tesoro was interested. He was stepping forward with his head low, he was holding himself as if ready to draw back in an instant; he was more curious than cautious.

Anatasia shouted, leaped from Comanche, ran and ducked under the fence, picked up a stone. She flung it at the big red rattlesnake that immediately coiled and rattled, watching her with its shining little black eyes. She found another stone, aimed at its flat head. It jerked its head out of the way.

She looked wildly around for more stones, feeling frustrated that here in such a rocky place she couldn't easily find what she needed. The stones were all too big or too small and she picked up and hurled whatever she could find. She was too excited to aim well and the snake, tired of being bothered, uncoiled and started off as fast as it could.

148

Tesoro still wanted to see what this strange thing was. Anatasia scared him back and followed the snake. If she could find the proper-sized stone and bang it a good one on the head she'd have it before it crawled into some brush where she couldn't get at it.

It was going to get away and this she couldn't bear, for it might come back and Tesoro, apparently, had no proper horse sense about snakes. She knew of one colt that had died from a snake bite on the nose. She gathered more stones as she scooted under the fence. Her idea was to get the snake to coil, ready to strike again, for then it would be stationary. She hated the thought of stoning it to death, wished she had better aim and a better weapon, wanted only to finish it with one blow on the head.

The snake found refuge in a clump of greasewood, protected by low-growing branches where Anatasia could throw rocks at it for hours without damaging it in the least. Now the only thing she could do was to wait and watch so that it wouldn't vanish completely.

She knew perfectly well that rattlesnakes don't go around looking for something to bite, that a snake does not like to bother with people or animals, that when it strikes it does it instinctively with the idea of defending itself.

Without deliberately wishing ill to any living thing a rattlesnake could cause the death of any colt, human, or dog that moved too near it. The snake left alive in the vicinity of the mare and colt was a threat to the colt's life, so it had to be killed.

But how? It was safe in its brush refuge and all Anatasia could do was to keep it coiled and rattling. From time to time she tossed a stone into the brush and then the metallic buzzing would start up again with fresh enthusiasm.

149

Mia stood rigidly, listening and snorting, Comanche stood frozen where he had been when Anatasia leaped from him. The colt stood looking over the fence, eyes big and bright with interest, ears stiff with listening.

Some squirrel was making the quick bird-like call that signalled danger. Most horses knew what that meant and would proceed cautiously when they heard it. The little black colt had a lot to learn, Anatasia thought crossly, and tossed a stone at him by way of offering instruction. He ducked and shook his head and continued to be fascinated by the curious noise.

Anatasia was beginning to wonder how many hours she could keep a rattler coiled and rattling. She was beginning to think that for some reason Kiko and Amy weren't coming until late afternoon. The sun was growing hot where she waited, she would be thirsty and hungry before the snake would leave its fortress.

Finally, she busied herself by gathering together all the proper-sized stones within a reasonable distance. By the time she had a fair-sized pile of weapons and sat down to wait, the snake decided to go elsewhere. This time Anatasia had better luck and better aim. One bang over the head and the rattler was finished.

It occurred to her that she had been here for a long time, that Kiko and Amy might come along any moment, that she would be wise to get out of sight. A few minutes ago she would have been glad to see them, but now that she didn't need Kiko she wanted to continue being a self-appointed spy.

She considered taking a stick and scooping up the body of the snake (it still moved) and tossing it off into the brush, then decided to leave it, just for the fun of puzzling Kiko. Pleased with herself,

150

she jumped on Comanche. Still feeling squeamish, he snorted as, from a safe distance, he eyed the snake which looked alive to him. He was glad to leave and scramble up the mountain to the look-out place.

Anatasia didn't see Kiko or Amy. She saw a man riding along. He was riding Rojo, and he wasn't Mr. Brothers; nor, so far as she could see, was he any of the cowboys. Even from a distance Anatasia thought that he looked grim and purposeful.

Kiko and Amy had been having a difficult time. At dusk the night before, when they had slipped into the shadowy hay barn, they stayed longer than they had intended. Amy was filling one sack, Kiko another, pressing down the hay to take as much as possible. They had their sacks nearly full when Kiko straightened up.

"Listen!" he whispered.

Amy too heard the sound. Someone was coming into the barn.

She crouched, motionless with fear, keeping still as do small frightened animals. She could see no place to hide. The stack of baled hay was as solid as a brick building, it was not like a stack of loose hay into which they could have burrowed.

Kiko moved quickly. At the end of the stack from which hay had been taken a child could climb massive steps made of bales. They climbed hastily and crawled across the top on their bellies.

Amy was wondering where, so high up under the rafters, a hiding place could be found when, in the dimness, Kiko disappeared. She inched forward, holding her breath. His hands reached up and pulled her down into a neat little square hole. It was by a high window-like door into which hay was loaded from the outside.

151

Just then the barn was flooded with light as the person, whoever he was, found the light switch. The children blinked at each other. Amy noted with relief that Kiko had had the foresight to pick up their feed sacks and drag them with him.

Nothing happened. They could hear someone moving about. Cautiously, Kiko started to pull loose hay out of the sacks, planning to cover Amy and himself, but he felt that he was making too much noise. Something rustled very near to them. A black-and-white cat looked down at them. Its long white whiskers twitched. *"Meow,"* it said loudly, and Amy suppressed a nervous giggle.

"Kitty?" a man's voice said.

"Meow," the cat replied.

Kiko bravely dumped what loose hay they'd collected over themselves and they snuggled down gratefully. The man would think it was only a cat rustling the hay.

Amy was sure that an hour had gone by, and gone slowly, when they heard someone climbing up the haystack. They waited so tensely that their muscles were ready to jump. They couldn't tell how close he was coming, they couldn't tell whether he had spotted the depression in which they hid. They were not at all confident that the loose hay into which they burrowed was ample covering. Amy felt sickening shivers along her spine.

A soft solid something landed on her. She very nearly screamed and didn't know how she managed not to. Then, as she felt herself being walked upon, she realized it was their friend the cat. But she heard a human breathing. It wasn't Kiko, for he seemed to have ceased to breathe he was keeping so very quiet.

"Oh, cat, you again!" the voice muttered disgustedly.

The cat, suddenly frightened, scrambled up and out, hurrying away. After a very long time of nothing whatever happening, the man too seemed to be going away.

Later, the light clicked off. Kiko would not yet stir. He heard the door open and shut—too loudly, he thought. When Amy started to sit up he pushed her back. He was certain that this person, whoever it was, was waiting in the dark for them to emerge. The feeling that he might be grabbed by someone unseen, unknown, was enough to give him unlimited patience.

More time went by before Kiko's sharp ears heard the door open and shut softly. Still neither child dared move.

Finally, when Amy could endure it no longer, she whispered, "I've *got* to go home. My mother and father will be furious."

"Okay," Kiko agreed. "I'll wait longer."

By now the barn was so dark that Amy wasn't sure that she could find her way down to the barn floor. She was terrified lest she fall from the high part of the stack. She crawled slowly, feeling ahead with her hands, thinking uneasily that there might be mouse-hunting snakes in the hay. She pictured large hairy spiders, which, ordinarily, would not frighten her.

When at last her feet found the floor, her hands must now find the wall. Finally she pressed against that and moved, searching for the door. When she came to the door it would not open. She tried with all her might. It was a small entrance door, set inside the big sliding door. Either it was padlocked or firmly barricaded on the outside.

Next she tried the big door. It would not budge on its rollers. She struggled a little longer, was afraid to cry out, knew she must find her way back up through the blackness to Kiko. He would be scared too, if he heard her crawling toward him.

She got up on top of the stack again and lost her sense of direction. She had never been in so black a place. "Kiko," she whispered, as loudly as she dared. "I'm trying to come back. Where are you?"

She thought that his answering whisper came from the wrong direction. "Come this way."

When at last she reached him, she had to wait for her heart to stop pounding before she told him, "We can't get out. They've locked us in, I guess."

Kiko stirred. "Wait here," he said, and went to investigate. Amy fought a desire to hurry after him. It was so hard to hold still in the unfriendly darkness with no way to measure time.

Kiko crept back, not getting lost as Amy had. "They locked us in all right."

"What'll we do?"

"Wait."

"Kiko! I want to yell."

"Don't."

Kiko's hands felt for the high door above them. His fingers found the latch and Amy was able to see a little as the opening let starlight in.

"Oh, Kiko, but it's such a long way down!"

Kiko ignored her. He was stuffing the loose hay back in the sacks. When one was filled he leaned out and dropped it straight down. He dropped the other, waited and listened. Carefully he edged himself out, hung by his hands, felt the side of the barn with his bare feet. He dropped.

154

"Come on," he whispered.

Amy couldn't move.

"Aw, come on. *Pronto!* Do like me. I'll help. It's okay."

Gingerly, Amy crept out. She held tight to the sill with her hands, letting herself dangle down. "Let loose," Kiko hissed.

But she couldn't and her tennis shoes tried to find some hold on the wall. Then her fingers refused to hold and she went down. She landed partly on Kiko, partly on the sacks of hay. It was so easy that she wanted to laugh.

Kiko picked himself up, not in a humorous mood. "You go home. I got to go hide the hay."

When she reached home she found that she hadn't been gone as long as it had seemed, but it was nearly ten o'clock and her parents had been quite frantic with worry. Her father lectured her severely on the subject of children worrying their elders and her mother was so upset that she shook Amy and delivered a quick slap. "Where in the world have you been all this time?" she demanded.

"Only in the hay barn. We just went in to find a kitten," Amy sobbed. "One of the men accidently locked us in. We had an awful time getting out and I was scared."

"Don't you ever, ever go into that barn again!" Mrs. Fairfield admonished.

Amy went to bed in tears.

As it turned out, all this was a good thing. Amy's mother didn't really approve of physical punishment, and by morning she was so dismayed at her lack of control that she permitted Amy to go off with Kiko and the burro.

155

The night before, in the darkness, Kiko had hidden the hay sacks in the brush by the canyon rim. Now, in daylight, the two children were almost afraid to pick them up. They were conscious of a mysterious enemy who spied on them, apparently almost constantly.

"I don't know what to do," Kiko worried. "Maybe we can travel all the way through the brush with the hay, but it'll be hard and take a long time."

"Why did they want to lock us in the barn? Whoever it is wants to catch us awfully much."

Kiko shrugged.

Amy continued, "I just thought—that high door we went out. Someone will know we were in there after all and escaped that way. We left it open."

"No, I found a long stick last night and poked it shut. It isn't locked, but it'll stay shut if the wind don't blow."

"Oh, that's good. Kiko, *who can it be?* We'd know if it were Mr. Brothers again, and if it were someone else, wouldn't your father tell you?"

Kiko shrugged again. "I think for a long time someone has been after us."

"Yes. It's so scary not to know who it is!"

They slid off Sancho and led him into the brush where Kiko had left the hay. They looked carefully in every direction first. If someone were watching them he was well hidden. However, so far as that went, there were endless places where someone could be hiding and spying on them.

156

"Now," said Kiko, having loaded the sacks on Sancho, "we just got to keep off the trail. The brush is going to pull the sacks off in some places. We got to go slow and maybe carry the hay ourselves part of the way. On Sancho it sticks out too far to get through close places."

It was hot and airless in the forest of greasewood and sagebrush. Kiko kept to the canyon side, picking his way through the tallest and thickest of the brush. Amy followed Sancho, watching his load. There were many stops and readjustments.

Above Black Horse Spring Kiko decided to leave Amy with Sancho and go down to look for tracks. He was not gone long. He returned to report breathlessly, "Someone riding a shod horse—looks like Rojo's tracks—rode down the trail. Before that there was someone on a barefoot horse, sort of dodging in and out of the brush. Golly, I don't know—"

"What'll we do?" Amy asked in a small voice.

"Just keep on going, I guess. We got to get this hay there if we can."

It was after they had gone through their own secret wire gate and started up the trail between the tall lilac that they grew badly frightened. Plain on their hidden trail were the tracks of a shod horse.

Kiko stared at them in dismay. Then he took the hay sacks and crept off into the brush to hide them.

"We'll look down in the clearing from the top of the trail," he told Amy.

They didn't know exactly what to expect but they knew that, whatever it was, it would be bad.

What they saw was worse than anything they could have imagined.

157

21

Wʜᴀᴛ ᴛʜᴇʏ sᴀᴡ was nothing. Absolutely nothing. The bars of the gateway were down and Mia and Tesoro were gone. From where Kiko and Amy stood they could see no living thing at all. Not even a rabbit hopped across the clearing. No bird sang.

Amy took a deep, frightened breath.

Kiko blinked, then looked at the trees and rocks and brush for a sign of motion on the mountain.

"Golly," he said despairingly.

They remained standing and staring, unable to think of anything else to do. Finally Kiko said, "Let's go down and look for tracks."

Amy recovered her speech. "Whoever's riding Rojo has to come back this way. So let's put Sancho in the corral and act as if we're playing there—looking for arrowheads or ollas or something, the way we told Mr. Brothers we were doing."

At least this was something to do.

Sancho was the first to discover the snake. His ears went high and rigid; he snorted.

"Now who came and killed a snake?" pondered Kiko. They put Sancho, still snorting, into the corral and Kiko walked carefully toward the dead snake, looking in the dust for tracks.

"Some barefooted kid," he said in amazement.

"And there go the tracks of Mia and Tesoro, up the mountain!" Amy gasped.

"And another barefooted horse. And then those shod tracks."

"Who?"

"Well, I guess Anatasia after all. But who rides Rojo?"

"Anatasia!" Amy exclaimed, disregarding his last question. "But what could she be doing?"

"Who knows? Oh! She must have found our mare and colt, she must have told someone."

"She wouldn't be that mean, would she? She wouldn't tell."

"But she did, didn't she? There's Rojo's tracks all right."

"Kiko, why would all the tracks be going up the mountain? If Anatasia told some man, and he got Mia and Tesoro, he wouldn't be going on the mountain with them. He'd take them back up to the ranch, to Mr. Richie. Wouldn't he?"

"Guess so. I don't know. All I know is that someone's stole our mare and colt."

159

"But how can we ever find them? We can't ask anybody anything. We aren't even supposed to know anything about Mia. We don't even dare look for her if we're being followed."

"We can't do a thing!" Kiko said desperately. "Nothing. We can't even go following these tracks to see what's happening. We got to pretend like we're playing around here. That Anatasia! She's a bad one. She's got us in trouble for sure."

"I just can't bear it," Amy answered. "After all this time—that they'd find Mia and Tesoro. And we really *can't* do anything?"

"Do anything? Well, what? What do you say we oughta do?" Kiko sounded angry.

"I just can't believe Anatasia would be so mean! After she seemed so good. She loved the little fawn so much—"

"She's an enemy," Kiko stated flatly.

"I suppose it's true. But what comes next?"

"Nothing. We'll play around here a little while and come back tomorrow. Come back lots of days. Wait and see, I guess."

"If we stay around here maybe Anatasia or that other one will come around. Maybe we can find out something."

"Maybe."

But no one came. Reluctantly, Amy decided that she had better go home.

Kiko went home too, and when his father came in he asked him, "Who's riding around on Rojo? I seen his tracks. Mr. Brothers didn't come back, did he?"

"No. Another fellow. Just came yesterday, I guess. I haven't seen him to talk to, but Mr. Richie said to leave Rojo in the corral for him, and he's staying in Mr. Richie's big house. Something about

160

the insurance on Mia. I guess the insurance company won't pay Mr. Richie for her until they send a man to look around and make sure she's gone."

Trying to sound hopeful, Kiko said, "Maybe he'll find her."

"I think maybe he won't. Like I say, if that mare was anywhere around here someone would have seen her by now. Anyway, he's going to look for her, like Señor Brothers did, I guess."

Kiko was too worried to eat very much supper and he didn't sleep well that night.

Amy was as confused as Kiko when, in the morning, he told her what he had found out.

"But if the insurance man has found Mia and Tesoro and has taken them, where are they? When he found them wouldn't he bring them right back up to the corral by the barn? I simply can't understand what's going on. I wish we could *see* that man. I'd feel better, really, if I could look at him. He must be the one who locked us in the barn. But why did he do that, unless he suspects us—and why should he?" Amy suddenly stopped talking. Then, her eyes wide, she asked, "Kiko, if this man just came, who else has been spying? *Who was the one before this man came?*"

Kiko could do nothing but scratch his head. "You ask too many questions," he said wearily.

The next few days dragged by.

Kiko and Amy couldn't feel hopeful as they traveled down the canyon. They didn't let themselves hope that Mia and Tesoro would be back in the corral again. But at least they didn't have to be furtive any longer. They could leave tracks in plain sight all the way to the hermit's clearing. Wasn't the clearing supposed to be their place to play? They rather hoped to be found there by whoever their sinister follower was. It would be a relief to face him.

Amy kept puzzling about what part, if any, Anatasia was playing in the mystery—if, indeed, Anatasia was mixed up in it at all. She couldn't agree entirely with Kiko that Anatasia was their enemy. She wished that Kiko would be less stubborn and would agree to go to Anatasia in order to try to find out what was going on.

Amy could feel a dark pressure of worry weighing her down. It made her feel desolate. It was her last sensation before she went to sleep at night. In the morning she awoke with an unhappy feeling, and as thoughts and dreams untangled she became more and more aware that she and Kiko did not know where Mia and Tesoro might be, what danger they might be in.

Anatasia who, ordinarily, loved excitement, was having too much of it just now.

She had thought it was exciting enough when she had first found the mare and colt. She had enjoyed being sly, covering her trail in devious ways, visiting the animals without letting Kiko and Amy know.

What had started to be an amusing game had turned out to be no fun at all.

When, from the look-out, Anatasia had seen the stranger on Rojo, she had scarcely taken time to think. She had leaped on Comanche and gone plunging down to the corral, had put a rope on Mia, and had ridden, leading Mia, with the colt following, up a brushy deer trail. She knew she was going to be followed and it was her aim, if she could, to lay plain tracks, then circle back. She had a dreadful feeling of certainty that the man on Rojo was out to find Mia. What else could he be doing? For what other reason would a stranger be riding around on the horse Mr. Brothers had used?

The mountain was wild and rough. There were areas of deep brush, gashes of small ravines and valleys, all, no doubt, known by the wild black stallion a hundred years ago. Anatasia herself did not know the mountain well, but she was accustomed to rough country, she could comprehend the lay of the land. Perhaps she could find a place to hide the mare and colt, a remote spot which the man on Rojo would not be able to find.

At first she traveled too swiftly, feeling panicked. She made the horses scramble up steep brushy places, she hurried across rocky ledges where no tracks would be laid. Then she realized that whoever might be following would not be likely to feel this desperate sense of urgency. The man, whoever he was, would be trailing doggedly along, sure of his quarry and therefore in no hurry.

She stopped to rest the animals while she tried to make some practical plan. She didn't see how she was going to spend the immediate future of her life playing this frantic game of hide and seek with a stranger. She couldn't drag Mia and the colt over the mountain all day and all night. There had to be a stopping place—and a safe one. Somewhere the animals had to be fed and watered.

She let the horses rest as long as she dared while she considered all this. Then, forcing herself not to hurry, she traveled in a large circle. Starting to the left, she climbed up through the brush. Veering to the right before descending, she came to almost the exact spot where she had rested the horses.

Plainly, she was being followed. There were the shod tracks laid

163

on top of Comanche's, Mia's, and the colt's. She cut across all the tracks, traveled on a meandering deer trail, got more scratches from the brush, circled again, picked up Rojo's tracks. Now she was tracking the rider who was tracking her. This, for the time being, was the only safe way to play it. From a cautious distance she must keep following the red horse's tracks until his rider gave up and went back to the ranch—or until she could think of somewhere to hide.

But how could she get herself and Comanche home in good time without being seen crossing Mr. Richie's ranch? What should she do with Mia and her colt? Though neither of them, originally, was her responsibility, they were now because she loved them.

22

IT WAS THE fourth day since Mia and Tesoro had disappeared. Early in the morning Amy and Kiko followed the tracks of Rojo all the way down the canyon, straight to Mia's corral. There they saw that the tracks went on up the mountain. Whoever it was could look down on them from their very own look-out. The knowledge made them speak in whispers.

"I'm scared of him, whoever he is," admitted Amy. "But I still wish he'd come and let us see him. Maybe he doesn't look as awful as I think he does."

"He'll have to come back this way. No other trail." Kiko put

165

Sancho in the corral for the purpose of covering what tracks were left of Mia and her colt, as well as to make it appear that the corral was the burro's property.

"Let's pretend we're looking for arrowheads or pottery," Amy whispered. Kiko nodded and they crouched by a boulder at the edge of the clearing. Kiko, with his broken knife, languidly poked at the earth.

"Wish he'd come down soon," he muttered uneasily. "I'd like to get it over with. I feel spooky."

It seemed an hour before they heard a noise in the brush and Sancho lifted his head and brayed a welcome to Rojo. Rojo's rider looked unfriendly. He looked much more like Mr. Richie than like Mr. Brothers, Amy decided. He stopped and sat looking at the children who stared back fearfully.

"What are you doing here?" the man asked.

Amy stood up and said with dignity, "I'm Amy Fairfield and this is my friend, Kiko, and that is his burro, Sancho. You are—?"

The man had not expected to meet with such self-assurance. "I'm Mr. Bashford·and I want to know what you kids do all the time. Why do you go into the hay barn?"

Kiko felt helpless, unable to know what to say, but Amy experienced such a rush of annoyance that it gave her courage. She felt grown up and knew that she must speak boldly.

"I can't see that it's your affair, but Kiko and I do go into the barn quite often, to look for kittens. Why do you ask?"

"What do you do here?"

"This is our secret place and no one should know about it. We play here and we look for ollas and arrowheads. What are you doing

166

here?"

The man looked irritated. "I'm checking on something. There are barefooted horse tracks and colt tracks all over this mountain."

Neither child said anything. Mr. Bashford glared at them. "Well? What do you know about these tracks?"

Kiko scuffed in the dust with his bare toe. Amy said, "Nothing. Probably they belong to that little Indian girl. She sometimes rides an old mare with a colt following along."

"Indian girl? Who?"

"I don't know what her name is."

"Can you get to the reservation from here? Over the mountain?"

"We never found a way. But then we never looked very hard. We just wish we could find a whole olla hidden in the rocks. Kiko did look for a way through once, but he couldn't find a trail. You can see where you want to go, but you can't get there because of those real deep, brushy canyons. Kiko gave up."

Mr. Bashford nodded briefly and rode on. After he disappeared down the brushy trail toward the wire gate, Kiko went up to the look-out and was gone for some time. Amy went into the corral and comforted herself by talking to Sancho and petting him.

This pretty little clearing on the mountain was so very lonely without Mia and Tesoro that it seemed to be an unfamiliar place. At least if she and Kiko didn't know where Mia and her colt were, neither did sinister-looking Mr. Bashford, Amy reasoned, and felt better.

Kiko returned and had a plan. "Let's look on the mountain now," he said. "I watched the man ride on up the canyon, like he's going back to the ranch, and if he gets sneaky and turns around and comes

167

back here, it'll take him awhile to get here. We can have time to look around."

They climbed on Sancho, and, without too much hope, started up through the brush.

Horse tracks were on every deer trail, it seemed. There were the fresh tracks of the shod horse, Rojo, and the dimmer tracks of mare and colt and the other horse, which Kiko assumed to be Comanche. All barefooted tracks were old tracks, laid down, perhaps, on the very day that Mia and Tesoro had disappeared.

"Surely Anatasia knows something," Amy suggested.

"I think so, but maybe no. Maybe Rudie or Kennie, or someone else. Maybe these aren't Comanche's tracks at all. Could be someone we don't even know about. Maybe they found our mare and colt and just took them. Maybe they really are stolen now, and far away."

"Maybe is an awful word," Amy said drearily. "Maybe anything!"

Kiko stopped to let Sancho rest. "No use following all these tracks, they just go everywhere. I guess let's head for somewhere high so's we can look all around."

"Go toward the reservation. What if we could find a way through? We could see Anatasia or the twins, ask some questions—"

Finally they came across tracks that didn't seem to be wandering so aimlessly but were going in the same direction they were. Rojo had been following these tracks, too. Then all tracks disappeared on a ledge of rock. When they were back on dusty earth again there were only Rojo's tracks.

Kiko laughed. "Someone fooled ole Mr. Bashford after all. Look, he's lost the trail."

"But so have we," Amy pointed out.

168

"Well, no good following Rojo's tracks. And if we cut back across the rock and look for where those others took off it will take a long time. Let's head on to where we can look towards the reservation. If Mia and Tesoro really went that way, we'll pick up their tracks again."

Soon there was no trail at all. They slid off Sancho and Kiko walked, leading him, pushing through the brush. The only trails they found were small ones made by rabbits and squirrels. "We got to get on some deer trail that goes that way," Kiko said as he stopped to rest. It was hard going through the tall brush and around boulders. Amy wondered how they would ever find their way back to the corral.

"You hold Sancho. I'm going to climb up on this rock and look around," Kiko announced, and seemed to go right up the side of a high boulder as easily as a squirrel would go. When he came down he shook his head disgustedly.

"This Black Horse Mountain isn't one mountain at all. It's a whole lot of mountains with those canyons between, and there's no way of getting to where you want to go."

"That's what I told Mr. Bashford. I guess he found that out, too."

"Let's keep going awhile longer anyway. Let's get up high and try to see a way."

It seemed hopeless, pushing on through the brush, but Kiko thought that in time they'd come across an opening or find a trail that the deer used. He was right. They felt a slope beneath their feet, came suddenly to where the chaparral grew sparser, found themselves looking across a brushy ravine.

But they couldn't fight their way down into it and up the other side. Kiko looked along the edge, on up the mountain, saw where

169

the draw ended, saw a ridge he called a hog-back connecting the rise of hills. He headed for it, traveling along the ravine rim where brush grew not so tall.

Then he stopped, delighted and amazed. "Here come all the bare-foot tracks again! And no Rojo tracks."

Encouraged at last, they followed the tracks which went exactly the way they wanted to go. Even Sancho moved more eagerly. From time to time he put his head down, tracking.

Amy was surprised. "I didn't know that donkeys or horses ever smelled a trail, I thought only dogs did."

"Yep," said Kiko. "Some horses are real good at it. They can help you find horses you're looking for out in pasture."

Ahead of them were more boulders, big as houses, Amy thought. The hog-back was a slanting shoulder, rising up on one side, joining the mountain, and all along it and the mountain were steep slabs of rock, solid as pavement, but rougher.

They were stopped by what seemed to be a formidable barricade everywhere but the way they had come. To their left the ravine dropped straight down in a cliff. Their way to the shoulder of the hog-back was blocked by a giant boulder with brush high around it.

They halted in dismay. "Where do the tracks go to?" Kiko wondered.

"They come here and they vanish, as if they flew off."

"Just tracks here, not going back, not going anywhere. If they went on, someone has brushed them out. But where could they go to? Golly! Where at on this mountain can Mia and Tesoro be?"

"Can you climb up anywhere and look?" Amy asked.

Kiko eyed the wall of rock that rose up the mountain where hill

170

and shoulder joined. He was starting to see how high he might be able to climb when suddenly Sancho's head and ears shot up. His nostrils flared, receiving some message from the air. His ears had never looked so tall and under their thatch of brow his button eyes had never looked so bright. He drew in his breath with a wheezy, rusty sound and let it out with the loudest bray the children had ever heard.

From far off, down somewhere below them, they were sure they heard an answering whinny.

Quickly Sancho pulled his rope from Amy's inattentive fingers. Head low, he hurried toward the big boulder. He nosed his way into the brush, then disappeared.

23

It wasn't one big boulder. It was two boulders with brush tall around them. Amy and Kiko pushed through the brush in time to see Sancho's tail vanishing down a slope. They ran.

Never had Sancho traveled so fast. The rope he still wore trailed swiftly along like an extra tail. Here the brush was not tall, the going not bad. Hurrying as he was, Kiko still noted the signs on the earth.

"Tracks do go this way," he panted.

Suddenly they stopped to look down upon a fallen-apart cabin, a rickety corral, a mare and a colt.

"But they aren't ours!" Amy wailed.

172

Kiko stood staring, saying nothing for a moment. "But Sancho thinks so. Look!" he exclaimed.

The little burro had reached the corral fence where both mare and colt crowded eagerly against it. Obviously, both were glad to see Sancho.

"But that isn't Mia!" Amy repeated. "That mare has a big white face. And white socks. And from here it looks as if that black colt has a star on his forehead. What's Sancho so happy about?"

"Golly! I don't know. Guess he just likes colts."

"How did he know where to find these?"

"Must have smelled them. He wanted to find Mia and Tesoro."

They proceeded down, not running now, walking rather sadly. As they approached the corral the mare whinnied to them, just as Mia used to do. The colt stood tall and said, "He-he-he!"

Kiko stopped and stared some more. "That's Mia's whinny. Oh, golly! That's them!"

"It can't be," Amy protested, but Kiko was hurrying again.

When she caught up with him he was laughing. "It *is* them! Someone's painted them all up!"

"Of course it is," Amy exulted, crawling through the fence to hug Tesoro. "Mia looks so funny, her head isn't even pretty with that big white blaze that spreads out over her nostrils. Makes her head look too big. But, oh, it *is* Mia! And Tesoro! I can't believe it."

"Sancho can."

"Darling Sancho! He found them for us. He found the way. How did he?"

"He knew we wanted to find them. And he smelled them. He knew we were on their trail."

"But who brought them here? Who painted them? Why?"

"I did." And Anatasia rode into the clearing on Comanche.

They stared at her in bewildered astonishment. She giggled. "You sure look funny standing there with your mouths open."

Kiko closed his and opened it again. "Anatasia! I knew it. Darn you anyway! What have you been doing with our mare and colt? Why didn't you tell us?"

"Well, how could I? I was too busy trying to keep them safe from that man. Did you want me to let him have them?"

"Oh, Anatasia!" Amy exclaimed. "You *did* save them!"

"You bet I did! He almost got them, and more than once."

"Anatasia, don't be angry. We're grateful. Kiko just was surprised and didn't understand."

"He shouldn't have kept a secret from me. I could have helped."

"You *did* help. Wonderfully. But you surely had us fooled for awhile." Amy laughed and Anatasia began to laugh with her. "I'm so happy," Amy said. "We were nearly worried sick."

"Of course you were. Gee, I have lots to tell you kids. But first we got to take the mare and colt to water. There isn't any here. I have to take them to drink twice a day. Boy, have I been busy! And I nearly got caught, too. How did you ever find the way off the mountain?"

"We didn't. Sancho found it. How did you?"

"By accident. I wanted to climb that boulder to look around, then I found it was two boulders behind all that brush. Or I guess really one boulder, only split, like it happens sometimes. Anyway, we came here. It was the safest place I could find in a hurry. Probably we'll have to find another place. I don't like that man."

"But he must have been told what Mia looks like," Amy pointed

174

out. "Solid bay with only a white star. Now he won't know her if he sees her. And I did happen to tell him that an Indian girl had a mare and colt. Wasn't that lucky? I had to say something, he was asking about all the colt tracks, and I just said the first thing I thought of."

Anatasia regarded her handiwork. "From a distance they look all right. But if he looked close enough he could tell. I did want to make them both pintos, but I didn't have enough stuff. I put a star on the colt—no one's ever seen him so it didn't matter—but I thought he ought to have some decoration too. What's his name, anyhow? I never know what to call him."

"Tesoro. It means treasure."

"Well, he is. I never saw such a beautiful one. Are you coming along to water them? It's quite a ways. My uncle used to live here but he moved when the spring went dry."

Amy wanted to ask a hundred questions. Besides being overjoyed to find Mia and Tesoro safe, she was extra pleased to discover that Anatasia was no enemy, was now, in fact, their best friend.

She thought of something else. "We won't have to go back all the way over the mountain. We can go home the easy way, along the road through the reservation."

But Kiko didn't approve. "That Mr. Bashford would think it was funny to see us coming from this way. And you know he's going to be watching for us. We told him we couldn't get through this way."

"Yes, but if we go back over the mountain, through all that brush and around, it's going to be awfully late before we get home," Anatasia answered. "My mother will be so mad I'll never get to come out again. And we might even get lost."

175

"Huh," snorted Kiko. "Sancho wouldn't ever get lost."

Anatasia stood thinking. "It would puzzle that man, all right, to see you coming from the reservation way, if he is looking. But anyway, he still wouldn't know how to find Mia and Tesoro."

"No. But he'd figure we'd found a way from the mountain to the reservation, and he'd start looking for the way too."

"Maybe not. Maybe no one will notice if you go home by the road. Oh, I think I have an idea!"

"I hope it works," said Amy, remembering that she ought to be home long before now.

"Where would anyone least expect to see Mia?" Anatasia asked.

They stared at her dumbly.

"Guess."

Amy shook her head.

Anatasia laughed. "The very last place they'd think to look would be right up on Mr. Richie's ranch. Is Mia broke to ride?"

"You bet she is," Kiko affirmed proudly. "She goes good."

"Well then, I'll just leave Comanche in this corral. I'll ride Mia, we'll stop and water them, and I'll ride along with you kids. It will give someone a chance to see me riding a mare with a colt tagging along. I won't let anyone get too near because I'm not supposed to be on Mr. Richie's place anyway, so I can pretend to get scared and head for home if anyone looks at us too much. Then that man would think it was my mare and colt he'd been following, and not Mia at all."

"It's kind of scary." Amy frowned and thought about it. "But it *is* a good idea," she concluded. "It would throw Mr. Bashford off the track a little."

176

Kiko said, "I guess Mia would go all right with just a half-hitch around her nose. We usually ride her with the hackamore."

"Anyway, I can try," Anatasia said. She turned Comanche into the corral, pulled off his bridle and hung it on the fence, caught Mia and let Tesoro follow her out. Comanche didn't want to be left alone and whinnied sadly as they rode off. Then he settled down to graze on what grass was left in the corral.

Mia didn't in the least mind being handled with only a loop around her nose. She was glad to go with Sancho, she was thirsty and knew she was being taken to water.

As they traveled along what was left of the road that had gone to the cabin and the corral, Kiko kept eying Mia's white trimmings. "It would be bad if anyone looked too close. What did you paint her with?"

"Partly with blackboard chalk I'd brought from school and partly with the white polish for my Sunday shoes. I ran all out of polish, though."

"I think my mother has some," Amy said. "We can keep touching Mia up. We're as good as gypsies, they used to paint stolen horses. Tell us what happened. Did Mr. Bashford chase you?"

"And what about the rattlesnake?" Kiko wanted to know.

By the time Anatasia finished telling about her adventures they had left the old road and had taken a narrow trail into a small draw. There was a spring there where Indian horses and cattle came to drink and mare and colt drank their fill.

"We can follow the road now," Anatasia said. "Then when we get near my house I know a way where we can circle clear around. I don't want the fawn to see us and start following. And Mama and

177

the twins might see us and ask questions. I think, though, we better tell the twins because they can help us. I have to take Mia and Tesoro out to graze a lot because I haven't any hay and most of the grass is gone in that old corral. The twins could help do that when I couldn't get away. Kiko, do you think you can get a little grain once in awhile?"

"Sure. It's easier than getting hay. Easy to carry, too, in a paper bag as if it was our lunch."

"We just might have to keep hiding them in different places until that man goes away."

"The trouble is," Amy worried, "that we'll never know when he might decide to come back again."

"We'll just have to take a chance on that; be sure and always know when the man is around again, and then keep moving the mare and colt," Anatasia answered decisively.

As they neared Mr. Richie's land Mia stepped eagerly, remembering her old home. Tesoro had had no ideas about the world beyond his mountain and he trotted along, looking at all the strange sights.

Kiko slid off Sancho and opened the wire gate that Mia had jumped so long ago. Amy's heart beat fast with fear, for here they were on the upper part of the ranch, riding boldly along with the mare and her secret colt.

But nothing happened. When the mares and big colts came running across their pastures to stare over fences Tesoro became slightly timid and stayed close by his mother. For once, Anatasia wanted to be seen riding on Mr. Richie's land and no doubt she was observed by various people. She hoped that Mr. Bashford was watching from somewhere.

178

They rode quite near the ranch houses and then Anatasia deemed it wise to ride away. She didn't hurry. She wanted everyone to have a look at an Indian girl riding a bay mare with a blazed face and white socks, being followed by a black colt with a white star.

The next morning Amy and Kiko got on Sancho and rode down the canyon as far as the spring. Then they climbed up the canyon side, circled back to the upper part of the ranch and headed, by way of cow trails in the brush paralleling the road, toward the reservation. All this roundabout way of going was in the hope of confusing Mr. Bashford, should he be watching. They saw nothing of him, however. Rojo was in the corral by the barn.

"It'll be fun to see the fawn again," Amy said. "I bet he has grown."

He had. They found him wandering about at Anatasia's heels. He had decided that of all the humans he knew, Anatasia was the one who belonged to him. Again he let Amy pet him and cup his little black nostrils in her hand.

"Go catch Comanche," Anatasia ordered her brothers. "I'll tell Mama we're going riding, she won't care. Maybe she'll make us some sandwiches. Come on, Amy." Amy was delighted that the fawn went into the house with them. His small hoofs clattered on the kitchen floor.

Anatasia's mother welcomed Amy warmly. She put the girls to work rolling tortillas around beans while she found paper bags to carry them in.

Comanche was bridled and ready, standing patiently beside Sancho.

179

"We'll ride the horse and you girls ride the burro and carry the lunch," Rudie commanded. With the three little boys on his back Comanche looked heavily burdened, but Kiko said they'd all get off and lead the animals up steep places.

At first Rudie and Kennie had scarcely been able to believe what Anatasia, after swearing them to secrecy, told them. She might be making all this up, just to tease, and they eyed her incredulously. It seemed like a fairy tale, all so improbable.

Finally, convinced, they were eager to see mare and colt, they were delighted with the prospect of helping to hide them, helping to feed them.

The road seemed to wind up the hill as unambitiously as Sancho and Comanche traveled, but, if the children hadn't been so impatient, they would have considered it a pleasant slow ascent with great live oaks spreading shade. They passed two houses where dogs barked and children waved at them, then the road became more narrow and looked more unused.

Amy worried the whole way. What if someone had found this new place? What if Mia and Tesoro were gone again? But they were there, and Mia whinnied her greeting, a little louder than usual, for she was hungry. Tesoro echoed her.

"We have to get them out to graze right away," Anatasia said, sliding off Sancho.

Rudie and Kennie simply stared and said, "Gee" and "Golly."

"There's a nice little cienega with bunch grass where I take them," Anatasia explained while she put a long rope on Mia and led her out with Tesoro at her heels. They went through the brush, following a narrow trail, and there was the meadow where water, under

180

the surface, kept bunch grass thick and green. "After they eat awhile we'll take them for a drink."

Sancho and Comanche started enjoying the grass as if they were as hungry as mare and colt. The twins announced, almost in one voice, that they were hungry too, so the children sat in the shade and ate their lunch while the animals pulled bites of grass. The twins said that they had never seen so beautiful a colt as Tesoro. They could hardly believe it yet—that Kiko and Amy, no bigger than themselves, had fooled a number of grown people. How brave they were, and wonderful.

Anatasia planned how she would filch carrots and apples and sugar from her mother's kitchen. Rudie dreamed of what a great black horse Tesoro would be when he was grown, Kennie considered that Mia's legs looked as if she'd be able to jump over anything, and thought what fun it would be to take her over a hurdle. Once he had seen a horse show.

"One thing we should do today," Anatasia said, "is to go back up the trail and wipe out all the tracks there by the split boulder where we came through from the mountain. And push the brush back the way it was. We don't want that man to find the way. After he goes away and Mia and Tesoro are back in their old corral, it'll make a good secret trail for us kids to come from our house."

Amy said, "What if Mr. Bashford starts looking all over the reservation, comes in by the road?"

"He already has. There were some days when he was going all around everywhere," Rudie offered.

"He was!" Anatasia exclaimed. "I never saw him."

"That's probably when you were on the other side of the mountain. You found the mare and colt over there while the man was looking for Mia here."

"Oh, that's good. Now he can look all over the mountain when we have them here, and if he starts looking here again, we'll take them back there. He can't be everywhere at once. But we almost can because there are five of us and only one of him. We'll just have to know where he is all the time. Kiko and Amy can keep watching him while we look after Mia and the colt. Then, if he gets over this way, we'll move them again, and we'll watch him while Kiko and Amy take care of Mia."

"But what when school starts?" Amy asked anxiously.

"That's a while yet. He might give up before then. He can't look forever."

"We never know. He might come back."

"I won't go to school every day," Kiko announced.

"How come you won't? You have to have a note from your father after you go back, and if you stay out too long the school nurse comes."

"It's easy. I do it lots of times. I wake up coughing or with the headache and I feel too bad to go. Then, after my father goes to work, I get on Sancho and go where I want. I get back before he comes. And next day, or day after, I go to school, and he writes a note for me."

"One trouble is," Amy reasoned, "we won't know for sure the minute Mr. Bashford is gone. He keeps his car in the garage with the door shut and there's no way to peek."

"If he didn't have lights in his room at night he'd be gone. I been watching," Kiko said.

182

"But he just might go somewhere and be back the next day. And I don't believe he ever talks to Kiko's father, or any of the cowboys. He's lots worse than Mr. Brothers. I kind of liked Mr. Brothers."

Kiko giggled, remembering Mr. Brothers' mishaps. "This guy, he's real careful. Knows how to ride Rojo."

"Is Mr. Richie really so mean?" Kennie asked.

"I guess so. I haven't seen him very much." Amy tried to think of what she knew about Mr. Richie. "I guess my father and mother think he's all right."

"My father doesn't like him much," Kiko said.

"He couldn't be very nice, to have a new colt killed."

"Of course he couldn't know what Tesoro would be like," Amy offered, "but anyway, it wasn't very good of him."

"Rich people are like that," Rudie said wisely. "He'll probably send us to jail if he finds out."

"But we aren't doing anything really wrong," Amy said stoutly. "What's wrong about saving a little colt and taking care of his mother?"

They knew there was nothing wrong about this. Except in the strange and complex world of grownups, which, to the children, seemed not very reasonable.

24

I<small>T WAS EVIDENT</small> that Mr. Bashford wasn't going to waste time being friendly with anyone.

Back in the city Mr. Brothers had been talking to Mr. Bashford, whom he knew slightly. Mr. Brothers had taken it upon himself to tell the insurance investigator what he had learned about the case of the missing mare. He had the mistaken idea that he was being helpful to his cousin, Carver Richie, who, as a matter of fact, had no desire to have him do this favor.

After listening to Mr. Brothers, Mr. Bashford decided that it was not wise to talk to too many people on the ranch, ask questions of every Tom, Dick and Harry. Mr. Brothers had allowed himself to be sidetracked and confused, a mistake which Mr. Bashford was not going to make. In this way he did make a mistake. Had he asked questions he might have discovered that no Indian girl owned a mare and colt.

His first plan had been to keep an eye on the children, and he had followed that plan only to learn nothing of any value. He was wise enough to realize that children like to be secretive about unimportant matters, at least matters which adults knew to be unimportant. The boy and girl might be truthful in asserting that the place on the mountain by the old corral was their secret domain where they went to search for Indian relics. And it might be logical that they haunted the barn to look for kittens.

Yet, if they were as innocent as they seemed, he wondered why they appeared so cautious and furtive. And why did he feel as if the kids were always watching him from somewhere, even when he couldn't see them?

In a way, Mr. Bashford could understand Mr. Brothers' confusion.

He pondered what he had heard from Mr. Brothers: that the mare had got herself bred too young, that the sire was some scrub stallion from the reservation. This mishap should decrease the value of the mare, she might not grow well after producing a foal at so early an age. It was quite possible that she had died foaling. It could be that the mare lay dead somewhere, perhaps on the reservation, and Mr. Bashford looked for the remains of a dead mare.

He had the use of one of the ranch pick-ups, and occasionally, tired of Rojo, he drove about in that. On this particular day he followed the reservation road as it grew rougher and rougher, he bounced along to a shack and corral which seemed to have been used lately. Its gate was open. Mr. Bashford left the truck to follow tracks on foot. Mare and colt tracks went along a trail into the brush and Mr. Bashford followed the tracks to a clearing. From behind a clump of greasewood Mr. Bashford looked at an Indian girl who sat in the grass, holding a grazing mare by a rope.

There was a colt grazing, too, and a brown gelding. These were the same mare and colt he had seen with the girl before. It was a well-built, long-legged mare, but she didn't answer the description Mr. Bashford had of a solid bay mare with only a white star. It was a beautiful black colt she had; both animals seemed too valuable to be in the possession of a poor Indian kid. Probably stolen from somewhere, Mr. Bashford thought as he made his way back to the truck.

A few hours later, after Mia and Tesoro had eaten enough grass to keep them nourished for awhile, Anatasia started back to the corral. She discovered Mr. Bashford's tracks on the dusty trail and found his tire marks by the corral.

She worried. This man might come spying around just when she was touching up Mia's white trimmings with the shoe polish Amy had brought her. Or he might come sneaking near enough to see that the white markings were artificial.

Tomorrow she must find a new hiding place for Mia and Tesoro.

The twins were in the yard chopping up kindling when they heard a wild sound of running hoofs. Anatasia, on Mia, came pounding down the reservation road. Tesoro was running at top speed, his tail straight up.

186

"Open the kitchen door, quick!" Anatasia yelled, and whipped around the corner of the house. She jumped off Mia and pulled her through the back door. The colt, confused, ran twice around the house before the twins could station themselves by the door and shoo him in after his mother. He had never been under a roof before and he didn't like it. Both mare and colt stood snorting and blowing while Anatasia spoke to them softly and tried to soothe them.

The twins stared, open-mouthed. This sudden arrival of Anatasia and the animals was startling, and certainly it looked funny to see a mare and colt right there in the kitchen.

"What happened?"

"That man's chasing me. He tried to get a close look at Mia and I had to hurry. Here he comes now! Jump out the back door and swish away those tracks."

"A good thing mama isn't home," Rudie said, and started to giggle.

"*Wipe out those tracks,*" Anatasia commanded.

Mr. Bashford, riding Rojo, was halfway down the road before he noticed that he'd lost the trail. He turned and rode slowly back, started into Anatasia's front yard. The dog, Cisco, hopped toward him on his three legs, barking and snarling so ferociously that Rojo, unnerved, shied and spun around and would not take another step into the dooryard.

"Hey, call off this dog," Mr. Bashford shouted.

He received no response from the house.

"Hey! Anybody home?"

Neither spurs nor slaps with the rein ends would induce Rojo to step into the yard. It was not so much the barking and growling

187

that alarmed him as it was the way the strange-looking dog hopped and bounced. He had not seen such an animal and did not care to exercise his curiosity. The more his rider urged him, the more he whirled and balked.

"Hey! You inside! I want to talk to you."

Finally an Indian boy stuck his head out the door. "Whadda you want?"

"Say, did you see a girl riding a mare with a colt running along?"

"Naw." The head vanished, the door slammed shut.

The man didn't go away at once. He kept riding Rojo up and down the road in front of the house while Cisco made lunges at him. And then a fawn crashed out of the brush and Rojo bolted. The man, yelling "whoa" and pulling on the reins, rode a great deal faster than he cared to. He disappeared around a bend in the road.

Anatasia sighed. "He'll probably be back. But Cisco won't let him look in the kitchen." She was comforting Mia by feeding her the tortillas left over from breakfast and Tesoro crunched the apple Kennie offered him.

"How soon is Mama coming home, I wonder?"

"Not until late. She and Aunt Mary went clear down to the coast to visit a sick lady. And Papa's off chopping wood."

The kitchen was small and even Tesoro looked big in it.

"Let's hang a blanket over the window so if they look out they won't see Rojo and whinny at him," Anatasia suggested. "This is a swell place to hide them for today, anyway."

Presently Kiko and Amy came riding along on Sancho. "Rudie, you go out and tell them to tie up Sancho and come in here real

188

quiet," Anatasia ordered.

"What's wrong with Mr. Bashford?" Amy asked as Sancho halted. "He was coming down the road at a dead run—until Rojo saw Sancho and stopped so quick that Mr. Bashford nearly went over his head. Then he didn't even speak to us. He just looked mad and rode off into the brush."

"I guess Cisco and the fawn scared Rojo. Tie Sancho up and come in real quiet. We got a surprise in the kitchen."

"Can the fawn come in, too?"

"Yeah. Let him come. But make Cisco stay outside. He has to be on guard."

By this time Mia and Tesoro had calmed down and even seemed to like being inside the house with people. They didn't bother to whinny when they saw Kiko and Amy; they were too busy eating tortillas at the kitchen table. Anatasia filled the sink with spring water so that they could drink when they liked.

"Oh," cried Amy, when she and Kiko had recovered somewhat from their surprise. "You have the very best house! I never before was inside a house with a mare and colt and a dear little fawn. What will your mother say?"

"Plenty," offered Rudie.

"Only she won't know," explained Anatasia. "We'll have them hidden somewhere else and everything will be all tidied up before she comes home. Listen! Cisco's barking again! Go peek out the front window. I think Mr. Bashford is back."

He was. At intervals all the rest of the day he appeared and disappeared. When the children thought he was gone at last, Kiko got on Sancho and scouted around to make sure that he wasn't hiding

189

and watching from some brushy hill. Kiko tracked him back to the ranch, then returned to report that it was safe to take the mare and colt to graze.

By that time Amy knew she had to go home and she gave Tesoro a farewell hug. He was a funny little colt. He enjoyed it when Amy put her arms around his neck and squeezed him tight. She might not see him or Mia for a few days as she and Kiko planned to keep a watchful eye on Mr. Bashford.

As suddenly as he had appeared on the ranch, Mr. Bashford seemed to have vanished. At night Kiko noted that there was no longer a light in Mr. Richie's house. Rojo didn't stay in the corral by the barn; he had been turned out to pasture. But the children felt no great sense of relief. Because Mr. Bashford was capable of reappearing at any moment, they were as uneasy about his departure as they had been about his arrival. At least when he had been around they had known when to be wary.

Kiko spoke to his father. "That man must have gone away."

"Guess so. Never said good-by. Golly! He never said hello, either."

"He must have been looking for Mia, like Mr. Brothers."

Frank shrugged. "That mare, she's long gone. I don't know—it was a funny thing."

Kiko agreed.

After a few days, the children decided to take Mia and Tesoro back to the clearing on the mountain. After all, it was the safest place for them, now that Mr. Bashford was gone—at least for the time being. No one else had found the spot. It was easier to feed and water them there, and it was an easy place for Kiko to reach

190

quickly. Kiko was the one most likely to be free always to go to them; the others could never know in advance when parents might interfere with their plans.

The children were right about Mr. Bashford. He had been called back to the insurance office in Los Angeles, but he did plan to return. Mr. Richie had invited him to come back in September during deer season. Mr. Bashford liked to hunt and he looked forward to bringing down a buck. He had seen plenty of deer on Black Horse Mountain. Also, when the children were back in school and that Indian girl couldn't gallop away from him on that long-legged mare, he would be better able to continue his investigation. If he actually did find the mare alive, the insurance company would not have to pay Mr. Richie's claim and would save a tidy sum of money. Mr. Bashford's boss would be pleased.

Also, Mia's disappearance intrigued him personally, as did the fact that the Indian girl was in possession of a really fine-looking mare and colt. In a vague way Mr. Bashford had begun to feel that there was some connection between the disappearance of one mare and the appearance of another. He would look into this further upon his return.

25

BLACK HORSE MOUNTAIN was not a very grassy place. The children had to search for little hidden clearings in the brush where there would be feed for Mia and Tesoro. In certain places under the earth, stone or hard adobe had formed natural reservoirs that held water left over from winter rains. In such places clumps of bunch grass grew green. These tiny meadows, or cienegas, made ideal horse pastures. In places they lay like chains of lakes, grassy spots between clumps of thick brush, with narrow, grassy lanes leading from one to the other. The deer enjoyed these small clearings as much as the horses did. The children saw where does and fawns had bedded in

192

the grass.

The Indian children's fawn was growing fast and one afternoon he would not be chased back to stay in their dooryard. With Cisco, he followed his human friends. Amy was delighted to see him, though Anatasia thought he should have stayed home. "We'll have to go back earlier; he'll be hungry for his milk."

But the fawn, pleased to be with the children, didn't seem to miss his goat mother. He nibbled on leaves and grass, drank from the spring, and took a nap in the shade.

Tesoro was entranced with him and nuzzled his soft coat. He felt kinship with this creature who, like himself, was still very young.

The colt was continuing to find life more and more interesting. His world had expanded when he had met the Indian children and their horse and dog and fawn. He liked to wander around and graze with the brown horse, Comanche. He had no way of knowing that Comanche was his own father, but he admired him in the way that colts admire adult horses. Like most geldings, Comanche had forgotten that he'd ever been a stallion. However, little colts interested him and he was fond of being near Tesoro.

Mia was long past the stage of worrying lest every creature harm her small son. She enjoyed the times of grazing. She was growing a little lean from producing milk and the bunch grass tasted delicious as she pulled big mouthfuls of it.

It was nearing September, and the bott flies had come to bother the horses.

Amy was alarmed. "There's a bee after Tesoro!"

Tesoro stamped and switched his tail, then ran to his mother, rubbing against her in an attempt to rid himself of the pest. Mia

193

tilted her head, listening to the buzzing, and struck at the insect with a quick front hoof.

"That's not a bee," Kiko told Amy. "That's an old bott fly." He watched the fly hovering and zooming as it attempted to lay tiny golden eggs on the ends of the hairs along the animals' legs. Swiftly Kiko's hand shot out and the bott fly was no more.

"But it looked like a bee," Amy retorted.

"I guess," said Anatasia, "horses are supposed to think they are bees so they will be afraid of them and try to keep them from laying all those eggs on the end of their hairs. My father says the horses get the eggs inside them, and they hatch into worms."

Sancho stamped and waggled his ears and switched his tail at the flies. Comanche and Mia hated them and stomped and struck and tried to rub them off on each other. Little Tesoro simply could not endure the buzzing. He ran, he rolled, he rubbed on the others, he squealed with annoyance. He stamped, kicked, struck, shook his head in misery.

The children crouched among the animals' active legs, trying to kill the botts. They were hard to catch for they soared, changed direction very fast and swooped from one horse to another. Stalking bott flies was exciting as one had to watch out for quick-moving hoofs.

Suddenly the colt seemed to get the idea that it was no use trying to wish bott flies off on his mother of Comanche or Sancho. Instead, he ran to the nearest child and tried to hold still until his tormenter was caught. At first the children thought his behavior was more or less accidental, but when he repeated it time and again they decided he knew exactly what he was doing. It seemed to them that he was being much smarter than the older animals. Not even Sancho, who

194

was so wise, ran to Kiko for help.

"Summer's nearly gone when the ole bott flies come," Rudie said mournfully.

"Fall is bad," Kiko agreed. "When so many people are in the hills hunting deer we get fires sometimes."

"Fires?" asked Amy, alarmed.

Anatasia explained. "There's usually a big brush fire somewhere every fall. You can see the smoke coming up over some mountain. Sometimes they burn for days."

Kennie said, "Maybe I'll join the Forestry and be a fire fighter when I grow up."

"I'll get to be a paratrooper and make jumps to the fire line," Rudie chimed in. "Or I'll fly the plane that pours the stuff down on the fire to put it out."

"But what if fire came here and we were in school?" Amy asked.

They all agreed that this would be very bad indeed.

A fire was a danger the children had not considered. Until now they had had worries only about someone finding their mare and colt and about how to take care of them when school started.

"Do fires come fast?" Amy wanted to know.

"Sometimes," Kiko answered her. "All this brush and grass, it is very dry. And in the fall the east wind blows. When fire starts then it goes every place."

"We'll have to do something before then. Somehow we ought to get money and really buy Mia. Maybe we should look some more for ollas? Or the hermit's money?"

Rudie said, "Oh, Anatasia will think of something. She mostly always does."

That Comanche should be brown, the color of a deer, Mia a golden-brown bay, and Tesoro a solid black, was an interesting puzzle to Amy. She had learned enough about horses by now to know that bay and brown are strong colors, that it was odd that Tesoro hadn't been like one of his parents.

She voiced her thoughts the next day when they gathered to feed mare and colt. "A black horse is perhaps the most beautiful," she mused, "and I like having a black horse on Black Horse Mountain."

"There really was a black horse once," Anatasia replied.

"I know. Kiko told me. He ran all over the mountain and in the canyon. He must have had a wonderful time."

"He made the ranchers plenty mad because their mares would get away and pretty soon the old black stallion had all the mares as wild as him and no one could catch him."

"What finally happened to him?"

"Maybe someone shot him. Or maybe he just died when he grew old. No one seems to know. But people remembered him for a long time and named the canyon and this mountain and our reservation after him."

"How he must have galloped through that canyon," Amy said, imagining the wild hoofbeats echoing.

"One of the homesteaders brought him all the way from Kentucky when he was only a colt," Anatasia continued. "He was a Thoroughbred. The man said he wanted to improve the horse herds around here, so that was why he turned the black horse out when he was

196

big enough. But then the horse went wild and was just like a real wild stallion with a lot of wild mares with him. The men would ride and ride, chasing the bunch when they wanted to catch colts to break. The old stallion knew places on this mountain to hide where no one could find him."

Rudie said, "All our horses on the reservation probably have him for a grandfather."

"More than a grandfather," Anatasia corrected. "A great, great, ever so great, grandfather, maybe. Because that was long ago."

"Oh!" exclaimed Amy. "Then Comanche would have his blood. Then Tesoro! *Of course!* That's why he is so beautiful and so black and looks so valuable. That wild Thoroughbred was his very own ancestor!"

Kennie stared at the colt, an amazed look on his face. "Why, he's what they call a throw-back! I bet he's going to look exactly like that old black stallion used to look!"

They all stared at the little black horse who, nose to nose with his sire, was grazing on the thick clumps of bunch grass.

"He really *is* a treasure!" Amy exclaimed. Her mind was busy with the most entrancing thoughts. She could imagine the great wild stallion in his mountain empire, tossing his thick forelock from his eyes, always watching for men who were his enemies, knowing when to run, where to hide, being careful about going to drink at the spring. "And now the mountain has another wonderful black horse!"

The children, still staring at Tesoro, nodded solemnly.

Presently, Anatasia said, "I wish, somehow, the wild black one could still be around so's he could show Tesoro all the good places to hide. And Tesoro could be the new wild black stallion! Maybe

197

always and forever free on his mountain."

Kiko was more practical. "It couldn't be that way any more. Too many fences. Why, he couldn't even go into Black Horse Canyon without someone to open a gate for him."

"Well, anyway, somehow we've always got to keep him safe from Mr. Richie."

Kiko sighed. "I wonder where were good places where the wild stallion hid. Maybe we could hide Mia and Tesoro there, turn them loose when winter comes."

Anatasia thought that, turned free, the mare and colt wouldn't stay in a safe place. "We've taught them to be too tame. They like people, they wouldn't hide from anybody, not even Mr. Richie. I've been thinking. Maybe if we got some coils of wire here and fenced in some of the grazing spots where there'd be places to drink in rainy weather, then maybe, if we couldn't get here for a couple of days, they'd be all right."

Amy thought this was a good idea.

Kiko pointed out that it was difficult enough to get hay and grain to the hiding place, let alone hauling wire that would be hard to get in the first place.

But Anatasia persisted. "We wouldn't need fence posts. We could fasten the wire to the brush. Lots of scrub oak and manzanita that's plenty strong."

"But what if they'd get into it, get tangled?"

"We'd tie little white rags to the fence so they'd be sure to see it and not run into it."

"But what if they tried to get out?"

"They wouldn't. They don't try to get out of the hermit's corral."

198

"Then they'd have grass and we wouldn't need to bring so much feed," Amy suggested hopefully.

"The grass in a little fenced-in place wouldn't last long," Kiko reminded them.

"But we could move the wire and fence in another piece of grass." Anatasia was loathe to give up her idea.

"Well, maybe." Kiko looked skeptical.

"Anyway, we've got to think of *some* way to keep them when it's going to be hard to get here," she told him.

"School will be starting pretty soon," Rudie reminded them.

Amy was optimistic. "We've been lucky so far. Things just can't go wrong now. We'll think of some way."

Anatasia, Amy had discovered, was always on her side. "We'll have to," she agreed.

"But what if we're all in school and Mr. Bashford comes back? And finds them?" Kennie wanted to know.

"We'll keep painting them up and hoping he won't look too close. Well, what else can we do?" Anatasia asked, goaded by the expressions on the faces of the three boys.

Amy said drearily, "I don't even like to think about Mr. Bashford. It doesn't do any good."

"Well, maybe he won't come back." Anatasia shuddered. "He's like some dark dreadful Thing waiting to pounce. Until he gets here we just can't worry all the time, can we?"

"Golly, no," Kiko affirmed. "Anyway, I can always ditch school and do something if I have to."

"I don't suppose they'll put us in jail," Kennie said, not too hopefully. "We're too young. It'd be reform school."

199

"I knew a guy they sent to reform school," his twin answered. "It was plenty rough he told me. Jail's really better."

Amy had been thinking of something else, dreaming her dream about the wild stallion. "It's all so wonderful," she exclaimed. "We just found out something we never thought about before. Tesoro is really and truly a splendid, valuable colt. We always knew that, but now we know it even more. It is so exciting to think that here where the wild one really lived we have Tesoro, of his very own blood. Tesoro is really special! He is the one, of all the colts, that happens to look just as the black stallion must have looked. I was thinking about that—remember, Kiko? That time we climbed to the mountain top, and Tesoro looked so pretty, and I said something about the old wild horse. But I didn't know then that Comanche was a descendant of his. You didn't tell me that, Kiko, or that the black stallion was a Thoroughbred."

"You didn't ask me. Anyway, Mia's valuable, too," Kiko answered her.

"Of course. Well, what I think is that we'll just do anything in the world, no matter what. We'll just do *anything* to keep Tesoro safe. Won't we?"

"Sure we will!" Anatasia, Rudie and Kennie answered in chorus.

Kiko, the practical one, said, "Sure, but *what?*"

No one yet knew the answer to that.

26

Kᴵᴷᴼ ᴀɴᴅ Aᴹʸ explored one of the storage sheds on the ranch.
There were many rolls of new barbed wire, but each roll was impos-
sibly heavy. Kiko shook his head. "I guess the only way would be
to unwind some, just enough to coil up and carry. Maybe a little
from each roll so's it wouldn't be noticed. But I don't know when
we could do it without being caught. Usually they lock this place
up at night."

"Couldn't we break off brush and pile it up? Couldn't we make
fences without wire?" Amy asked.

"It wouldn't hold. And it would be an awful job."

"Well, maybe it won't be too wet or cold this winter. After all, there are five of us now and somehow or other one of us ought to be able to see to the horses—one of us each day. For five days of school every week."

Kiko was concentrating very hard. He considered the fact that they got off the school bus at about three-thirty every afternoon. A hurrying child could reach the hide-away by four-thirty. It should take only a few minutes to feed and water the animals and to see that all was well. "Whoever went could maybe get home between five-thirty or six. In winter it would be dark, though."

"My parents are good but not that good," Amy stated, feeling sure that difficulties would be bound to arise if she were not in the house before dark. "And your aunt would have a fit if those kids didn't get in earlier."

"Anyway," said Kiko, "for awhile it will be all right. Until the days get too short and before the storms come. We better go now. I got two more sacks of feed hidden last night, we got to go haul them down. Someday we're gonna get caught—"

"We'll say we have a pet fawn hidden out, or something."

The first day of September came as a shock to Amy. She was awakened by a great sound of guns. She jumped out of bed and ran to the window. Outside, Mr. Richie and some friends were in the fields killing wild doves.

"Oh, oh, how awful!" Amy wailed.

"There's nothing you can do about it," her father told her later. "Some people like to hunt."

Amy began to cry. "There're baby doves in the nests."

"Of course not. They wouldn't have open season at such a time."

202

"Yes," Amy insisted, "yes, there are babies in the nests. We see them all the time. Two little gray babies in each nest. And they'll kill their mothers and fathers and they'll starve."

She was still upset when Kiko and Sancho came along. She asked Kiko anxiously, "Will there be hunters down the canyon?"

"I don't guess they go down there. Most of the doves are up in the fields."

As they traveled down the trail Amy thought how pleasant it must have been in the days of the wild black horse, before there were cars and men going about with guns. Of course people had hunted for meat in those days, but there weren't so many people in the country then and they couldn't travel so far or so fast. Now Anatasia said that the city hunters even got on the reservation where they weren't supposed to be.

Anatasia didn't come to the horses all that day. "She's out watching dove nests," Rudie explained. "When the babies get hungry and the big birds don't come, she knows they been shot. Then she tries to feed the babies bread and goat's milk."

"They always die anyway," Kennie said. "It's different from the milky stuff their mothers and fathers feed them."

"One lived once. It was older, almost all feathered out."

"What did she do with it?" Amy asked.

"She let him go after he could fly good. Mama was afraid the cat would get him."

These days when Mia and Tesoro could graze, they were saving quantities of hay. Kiko gave Mia one feed of grain a day because she needed it. Tesoro was doing well on grass and his mother's milk and both Sancho and Comanche had gained weight on the extra grazing.

After they had caught a few bott flies, the children sat listlessly in the grass. "Only ten more days till school," Amy reminded them. "One day my mother takes me to town to buy school clothes."

"My father says I got to wear shoes this year," Kiko said despondently.

"We have to, too," the twins lamented.

Fall was in the air. Goldenrod had started to bloom, oak leaves looked brittle and dry, some willow leaves had turned yellow. The squaw vine was bright red.

Summer had gone swiftly. "Anyway," Amy thought, "Tesoro's first summer was a good one."

Fearfully, she wondered about his second one.

Kiko asked the old question again. "How we going to keep on hiding them?"

"We just sort of wish and don't *do* anything," Amy said despairingly. "Once we thought we'd find ollas and make money and buy Tesoro and Mia. But we stopped looking. Now we ought to fence in grass, but we haven't."

"Anatasia will think of something," Rudie repeated.

As if he felt that his friends needed cheering, and as if he were positive that no bad thing could happen, ever, Tesoro suddenly leaped, then ran to bite at Comanche's knees. Comanche came down on one knee and reached out to bite and wrangle. Horse and colt reared up to spar, they dropped to their knees, they spun and flung kicks at each other. Comanche chased Tesoro and Tesoro chased Comanche.

"He's not worrying," Rudie observed, more cheerfully.

204

"Then we have to worry for him." But Amy dared to think that to so beautiful a colt surely life would be good.

He was not only their little colt—he also belonged to the great black stallion, he belonged to the mountain.

The twins were right. Anatasia did think of something. She came late one afternoon, the fawn with her. "Maybe you won't like my idea," she told Kiko and Amy, "but it seems to be the only thing to do. It's all I can think up, anyway."

"Well, what?" asked Amy.

"Comanche and Tesoro just love each other, you know. And nobody in the whole world knows that Tesoro is alive, except just us five kids. Next month he will be half a year old and that's old enough to be weaned. We could keep Mia in the corral and let him stay loose outside, he wouldn't go away. Then, when she went dry and wouldn't worry so much about him, we could take him home to live with Comanche. And you could sneak Mia back into the pasture with the other mares. Mr. Richie and all them would have a fit wondering where she'd been and how she got back, but they couldn't find out anything."

There was a long silence while everyone considered this.

Amy said, "I don't much like turning Mia over to Mr. Richie."

"It is bad, but what else can we do? I know there will be lots of days in winter when we just can't get down here, none of us. If it should storm real hard for days, like it does sometimes. Or if we'd get more snow than usual."

Kiko laughed. "It sure would be funny to see them start to train Mia and find out she's already broke to ride."

205

"It is a good plan but I hate them having her." Amy stared unhappily at the glossy bay mare and remembered when Kiko had first shown Mia to her. She remembered how shocked she had been that the colt was going to be killed. "You know, I think Mia has grown just in the few months we've had her."

"Horses grow for years," Kiko said. "Having a colt too young didn't hurt Mia at all."

"That's because she got plenty to eat," Rudie reminded them.

Kennie thought of something else. "But what if we take Tesoro home to Comanche's pasture? What would Mama and Papa say when they saw him there?"

Anatasia sighed. "That's the part I haven't figured out yet. I think we'd just have to tell Mama all about everything."

"Boy, we might catch it."

"Maybe not. Nobody on the reservation likes Mr. Richie. Anyone who ever heard about it would probably think it good and funny that old Mr. Richie got fooled by a couple of little kids. Indians wouldn't talk. They'd just laugh to themselves."

Kiko said, "I'd have to sneak Mia back at night. Then run away from the pasture real fast because all the mares would be running and whinnying and someone would come to see what was wrong."

"They'd see that she'd had a colt, by the look of her udder."

"What if they'd find him?" Kiko wanted to know.

"They couldn't prove anything. Mr. Richie wouldn't be coming over to the reservation."

"But my father would. What if he saw him?"

"He wouldn't know that he was Mia's. How could he? Mama could say that a friend gave the colt to us kids. Or that Papa bought him for us. It wouldn't be a fib to say that a friend gave him to us because a friend did. Mia is our friend and she gave him to us. Mama doesn't like for us to fib."

"You could see him and play with him as much as you wanted," Rudie offered.

"Sure."

"And it would be fun to have another black stallion on Black Horse Mountain. The wild horse would be glad if he knew."

"Yeah. Tesoro could gallop around with the Indian horses."

Amy had a quick, delicious dream. "Maybe my father could buy Mia for my birthday present. Or Christmas."

"I have a birthday but nobody's gonna buy me a mare," Kiko remarked sadly.

"You have Sancho, that's more than I ever had. You know, Mia will probably be happy back with the other mares, once she grows used to having Tesoro gone. And Tesoro will have a good time on the reservation with Comanche. Kiko and I can bring him grain out of Mr. Richie's barn. Poor Sancho will miss all this, though."

"We'll ride him when we go to see Tesoro. They'll still be friends." Kiko was beginning to look pleased.

"That's so," Amy agreed. "I still think it's bad to let Mia go back to Mr. Richie, though, when she should really and truly belong to us. But I suppose it would be better for her. She's be sure to have enough to eat, rain or snow or anything."

"What we got to think about," said Anatasia wisely, "is what is best for them. And this seems best. If it will work. Telling Mama about Tesoro, I mean."

"If it doesn't work, we're sunk."

207

"Not really. Because Tesoro wouldn't get killed by Mr. Richie. Mama maybe might be mad at us, but I bet somehow she wouldn't let Mr. Richie get Tesoro."

"Anyway, I bet we all get a good licking." Kiko was remembering past misadventures.

"That won't kill us."

Rudie said, "We'll probably all go to jail."

"I got to go home now," Anatasia told them. "I have three baby doves to feed."

"Are they going to live?"

"Maybe these will."

The fawn followed her as she disappeared down the brushy trail.

Amy and the twins and Kiko continued to sit in the grass, all of them busy thinking about Anatasia's suggestion. It seemed to be the best plan anyone had thought of yet. And it might work, though it was not altogether good.

Amy thought sadly that if Anatasia's plan worked, she'd never ride Mia again. This seemed unbearable. She didn't really believe that she'd receive Mia for a present, even if Mr. Richie would be willing to sell her when he had her back.

She broached the subject to her parents. "I wish I had a mare of my very own." She was thinking of the lightness of Mia's step, the feel of her galloping stride, the fun of flying over a hurdle. But there was more than that. There was the sweet, wise air Mia had about her, the way her ears and eyes were placed, the white star she wore, the gentleness of her.

"Why couldn't you let me have my own horse someday? That's what I want for my next birthday or Christmas present," she con-

208

tinued decisively.

"Oh, you do, do you?" her father answered. "We don't know how long we'll be living here."

"I wish for always."

"But we don't own our house, we're only renters. We're planning to stay only until I finish writing my book. I agree it's great here and we're lucky we found such a place to stay, but it's not for keeps."

"Do we really want to go back home?" Amy asked. "I don't want to."

Her mother was on her side. "I'm not sure that I want to, either. It would be fun, wouldn't it, to get a little place of our own somewhere near here?"

"Oh, wouldn't it!" Amy exclaimed. "Oh, let's!"

"Don't get so excited," her father cautioned. "We're only talking. I don't know what we'll do. We can't make any plans right now."

"But tell me, honest and truly," Amy persisted. "It could be, couldn't it? Maybe it could be that sometime we could live around here and I could have a mare all my own?"

"It isn't exactly impossible, but it's not a sure thing, either. Far from it."

"But if it is what we all want to do, why can't we?"

Her mother asked, "Amy, don't you ever miss home? Your school and your friends?"

"No. Do you miss the city?"

"I think not. Not really. Perhaps someday I could learn to ride a horse. Your father could teach me."

"Mother, you could! We could all have horses. We'd have such fun!"

"Hey!" her father exclaimed. "Wait a minute. You're dreaming too fast!"

"The way it is now," said her mother, "we never see Amy. She's always off with Kiko and the donkey. What'll you do, Amy, when school starts and you lose all this freedom?"

"It will be perfectly dreadful," Amy said so decisively that they laughed at her.

"Well, anyway, you'll get some new clothes to cheer you up. We've got to go shopping soon."

Amy was thinking that jeans were much more comfortable than school dresses. And that she'd learned more this summer from Kiko and the animals than she'd ever learned at school. Of course it was a different kind of learning but every bit as valuable. Perhaps more so.

She sighed and began feeling sorry again because it wasn't likely that she and Kiko would ever own Mia. It was as if a trade had to be made. To keep Tesoro safe they'd have to part with Mia forever.

It came to her that sometimes the things that you love have to be let go. For their own sakes they have to be let go.

27

As soon as school started the weather turned hot. "It always does this just when we go back to school," Anatasia sighed.

They rode the bus unhappily. It was early morning but not a breath of cool air came through the bus windows. Children squirmed in their new clothes, felt their shoes to be much too tight.

"Well, anyway," Amy whispered, "our parents can't expect us to stay in the house after school when it's so hot. Kiko and I can go down the canyon."

The children didn't learn much of anything the first few days of school. They felt too uncomfortable to concentrate. Amy's thoughts

211

kept wandering back to the mountain and Mia and Tesoro, wondering if the animals were watching for them to come. Tesoro always whinnied a shrill little call of delight when he saw them. The fawn would be lonely, too. He wanted to be with Anatasia all the time now and paid little attention to his goat friends.

At least the days were still long enough so that there was no hardship about going to the mare and colt after school. As Amy had predicted, everyone realized that it was too hot for a child to stay in the house while it was still daylight.

Kiko went into the feed barn at dusk and filled his sacks with hay. Amy helped him whenever she could. They took their sacks of hay to hide in the brush at the canyon's rim, to be carried by Sancho the next day after school. The trip down Black Horse Canyon with the hay was always nerve-wracking; they couldn't travel with any speed and they never knew when one of the ranch hands might come riding along. Kiko was beginning to look forward to October when they might start to carry out Anatasia's plan.

Even though the heat lingered until after sunset, the journeys down the canyon and up the mountain were not bad. When the canyon was in shadow the air was extra-sweet with the fragrance of sun-heated chaparral. Amy would miss these trips and she thought sorrowfully that if Anatasia's plan were successful, Mia would need to be treated like a stranger. When she was back in the home pasture the children wouldn't dare be seen petting her very much; someone might grow suspicious.

Though Kiko loved the mare and colt with all his heart, he would be glad when he would not have to work quite so hard for them. Now he worried about deer season which would start before September was over.

"But you said the hunters never get back where Mia and Tesoro are," Amy reminded him.

"They never did before. But they could."

"Where do Mr. Richie and his friends hunt?"

"Mostly in our canyon. Or over the ridge by the big canyon. I guess they wouldn't want to climb around on Black Horse Mountain. They go where it's easier."

"I hope Anatasia can keep the fawn safe when he grows up."

"She'll hide him somewhere."

Amy wondered dismally why people thought it fun to go out and kill things.

28

DEER SEASON AND the east wind started on the same day, on a Saturday morning when both the wind and the sun seemed to rise together. Clouds of yellow dust swept across the land, tumbleweeds went bounding along like strange, living creatures. The wind burned hot and dry.

Amy's mother said, "You aren't going off with Kiko today. I don't like this dust storm. Besides, the hunters are out and it will be dangerous in the hills."

Amy protested. "The wind doesn't blow down in the canyon. I don't think many hunters will be out today. How can they see

214

to shoot? I haven't heard a single gun."

"You can't hear because of the wind. Of course the hunters will be out. Nothing's going to stop them on the first weekend of deer season."

It was true that the wind made so much noise that nothing else could be heard. It ranted around outside the house, banging on doors and windows. "But it would be sheltered down in the canyon," Amy persisted.

"Then the hunters would be there, too. Why can't you stay home for once?" her mother sighed.

"Because Kiko and his cousins and the fawn are going down the canyon."

"Well, you aren't." Mrs. Fairfield closed the subject with finality.

Amy stared out the window. Even the sky looked yellow with dust. She watched the trees bend and shake, saw Kiko and Sancho, both looking miserable, coming along. She ran out into the searing wind and shouted to Kiko that she had to stay home. "This is a bad wind," he yelled, and rode on.

Kiko had told her how everyone hated the east wind. It was a hot wind in September and October, but when it blew in the winter it was icy cold. It wanted to wither everything, it was bad for new green grass, it could make springs go dry and wells give less water. Amy hoped it wouldn't hurt the spring on the mountain.

The wind died down toward evening, then started up again. Amy heard it in the night. The next morning it was still blowing, but, she thought, not quite so hard.

She looked out, to see Kiko coming as fast as Sancho could run. She hurried outside and Kiko pointed to the east, shouting something she could not hear.

Amy saw great clouds of black smoke boiling up to the sky. She began running as fast as she could after Sancho. Her father called to her to come back, but she couldn't hear what he said and she kept on running.

Halfway down the steep trail she caught up with Kiko who had had to stop to let Sancho rest. The little burro was puffing so hard his sides were heaving. Kiko said, "Hunters must have started a fire somehow, and the wind's behind it. We got to get to the horses quick." Without waiting for Amy to catch her breath, he started on.

When they reached the canyon floor Kiko let Amy ride the burro. He dog-trotted along beside them. At the spring he made Amy get off while he rode, and at the fence he didn't bother with the hidden gate they'd made long ago but hurried through the easier gate. "Now I'll lead Sancho up the trail and you keep him moving fast with a switch."

Never had they reached the hide-away so soon. And never had they seen so much commotion. Every Indian child and every dog from the reservation seemed to be there with Anatasia and Rudie and Kennie. Everyone was shouting at once and the dogs barked with excitement. The twins were on Comanche and Anatasia was holding Mia, who had her hackamore on. Tesoro was wild-eyed.

"I want to see how fast it's coming," cried Kiko, and leaped on Mia. He rode up the mountainside.

"How about your house when the fire comes?" Amy asked.

"All the men are out making a fire break. I guess we'll just have to take Mia and Tesoro there. Look! Here comes Kiko, down in a hurry."

216

Mia was plunging down the mountain, partly sliding on her haunches. Kiko yelled something. Just then the fawn appeared. "Oh," cried Anatasia, dismayed. "I thought I'd left him safe at home!"

"Listen," shouted Kiko. "We got to all run straight at the fire. You know that ridge? And that little place just out above the big canyon? There's a bunch of cattle there, and the fire's going to get them. We got to hurry them right at the fire, turn them up the ridge, cut across that little canyon and over into Black Horse Canyon and chase them on up to where it's clear."

"We never can!"

"We got to. With all the kids and dogs running at them, we can. Cows spook at people running on foot. You kids pick up sticks. We got to get them off the cliff. Come on!"

And he and Mia were gone, down the brushy trail, with Tesoro at Mia's heels. Comanche and the twins were close behind, Anatasia and Amy urged Sancho into a lope, and all the children swarmed behind them. The fawn went bounding beside Cisco who was managing remarkable speed on his three legs.

They all slowed down, then began to scramble up the east side of Black Horse Canyon. Amy noted fearfully that already the canyon was filled with smoke. When they reached the ridge, there was the loud roaring and crackling of the fire. It was so near they could feel its heat. Small gray burned leaves came with the smoke. But the smoke didn't settle as it did in the canyon; the wind that was blowing the fire toward them was carrying the smoke on. It was thick enough to make their eyes smart but they could see where they were going.

Amy was too frightened to observe with any interest the hurrying

217

deer, coyotes, foxes, rabbits and bob cats that came from the direction of the fire. The wild creatures had no fear of one another or of the children, the fire was all that they thought about.

Mia, with Tesoro sprinting behind her, was only a length or two ahead of the twins on Comanche. Sancho kept dropping from a lope to an up-and-down, bouncy trot. He did not have legs of the proper length for running far nor fast. To Amy, this feeling of needing more speed and being unable to obtain it was like having a nightmare in which you needed desperately to run but found that you couldn't. The tears that streaked her face were partly caused by smoke and partly by desperation.

It seemed impossible to get to the cattle in time. It seemed more likely that no living thing could escape the fire. Amy would have been even more frightened had she realized what Kiko knew—that wind can carry sparks to start a new fire some distance ahead of the existing one, creating a trap between two fires.

Children and animals hurried across a ridge, dipped down into a shallow canyon. It was over the lip of this canyon that, when rains were heavy, the waterfall dropped down and down into the deep canyon. It was on the rim of the great deep canyon that the cattle were going to be trapped.

Everyone slowed again, panting as they climbed the east slope of the little canyon. At the top of the slope they met the fire. It might have been half a mile away, but it was reaching its crimson arms toward them and sending smoke and ashes to blind and choke. The force of the fire itself was creating more wind.

Anatasia was trying to yell at Kiko to turn back, to tell him that it was hopeless, but he couldn't hear her above the roaring of fire

218

and wind. Amy peered through smoke, trying to see Tesoro. Where the fawn was she did not know. She saw a coyote, trying to hurry along, with one back paw missing. Like Cisco, the coyote must have once been caught in a trap. The sight made her look wildly around for Cisco but she couldn't see him either.

Now Kiko and Mia turned right, and vanished in a great puff of black smoke. "The fire found some greasewood," Anatasia tried to shout into Amy's ear. "Makes blackest smoke."

They were trying to hurry over rough stony earth, with the fire on their left and the deep canyon on their right. Anatasia pointed to the sky and out of the smoke Amy glimpsed a yellow plane which was dipping low. She could not hear its roaring engines but she saw the flash of red as fluid, to conquer the fire, was dropped from the sky. The wind seized it, scattered it, took it off and made it useless.

They turned even further to their right to follow the contour of the canyon rim, to circle the cattle which they could see through the smoke. The creatures turned smudged white faces toward them.

Kiko stopped to let Mia breathe, to get all the children together. "We got to run right at them," he shouted. "Turn them back the way we came!"

Bewildered beyond any sense, the cattle would not easily turn. Some tried darting back, past the children, to the cliffs. Kiko and Mia were everywhere, running, turning, stopping, getting this heifer and that one going in the right direction. Sancho bit with his long teeth at a slow-moving tail, Comanche worked like the good little cow horse he was. The dogs that were not too tired (one of them, Amy saw with relief, was Cisco) bit at heels and ducked to miss

219

flying hoofs. The children on foot, waving sticks, ran and yelled.

Yet, with all this, they could not get the cattle properly bunched up and moving. From the animals' point of view, they were being chased straight into fire and this was against their strongest instinct.

Kiko rode wildly and desperately. Time could not be wasted, the fire was coming too swiftly. In a minute or two, if the cattle could not be stampeded to safety, it would be too late to save them. The children would have to hurry to save themselves and their own animals. They were all on the edge of exhaustion. Kiko was not quite ready to give up. Mia's long legs carried him, he beat with his rope on rumps pointed the right way, on faces pointed the wrong way.

There was a sudden roar, heard even above the noises of fire. Down from the sky came the yellow plane, came screaming, too low for its own good, came at the huddled animals. Sancho was too tired to care, but Mia and Comanche had strength to shy without knowing surely which way to jump. The airplane seemed almost to stagger over the canyon rim, was helped by an updraft, righted itself, found a safe place in the sky, dove down again.

Now the cattle ran, and the children, with a surge of new strength, were not far behind.

Once started, the cattle moved willingly. What had made the rescue so nearly impossible was the necessity of driving them toward flames in order to get them off the threatened point of land. Now the heifers were glad to turn off the ridge, dip down and out of the shallow draw, plunge into Black Horse Canyon and hurry along the canyon trail that would take them to the upper part of the ranch.

220

Though the canyon was filled with smoke, though the children could hear the roar of the wind-driven fire, there was this interval when they could move a little more slowly, try to catch their breaths. So long as the cattle stayed ahead of them the cattle were safe; so long as the children and the animals kept moving they were safe.

Amy felt sudden and dreadful despair. She had been too excited and frightened to think of this sooner, but the fact was that all of them, Mia, Tesoro and the children, were soon going to meet Mr. Richie, Frank, Amy's parents, the cowboys, the sheriff, perhaps even Mr. Bashford. They were going to be confronted with all the adults whom they had been deceiving. Mia and Tesoro would be snatched out of their care. Their dream of raising a colt in a safe wild place was ending.

Had it not been for the bunch of cattle, helpless on the ledge, it could have been possible to hurry with Mia and Tesoro across the mountain to the reservation. If the Indians were out working on a fire break, surely there would have been some safe spot there. Perhaps they could have carried out Anatasia's plan of keeping Tesoro in Comanche's pasture and returning Mia to the ranch. It might have been a logical time, in all the confusion of the fire, for Mia to turn up safe at home.

But now the plan simply wouldn't work. They were all going to be caught because there had been no other way—they couldn't have left the cattle to be trapped by the fire.

The fire was being blown southwest. Soon it would climb down into Black Horse Canyon and roar up the other side, for fire climbs with speed up a brushy hill. Anatasia had been thinking that, with the wind from the east and slightly from the north, the fire would

221

cut slantwise across the canyon, leaning to the south. It would, of course, consume most of the canyon, but if they kept going they would get to the upper, cleared part of the ranch in time.

When they reached Black Horse Spring the cattle were frantic to drink. "Don't let them," yelled Kiko above the sound of wind. "Keep them thirsty and they'll hurry faster to get to water up top."

It took all the efforts of children whacking with sticks, and dogs nipping and barking, to keep the heifers moving along. Horses and Sancho were allowed to drink a little, dogs jumped into the big wooden trough and lapped, the fawn sipped some, but didn't like the taste of water stirred up by dogs. The children took a few swallows from the place where the water flowed clean from the pipe, then splashed water on their faces. They called the dogs and hurried on, fearful that the heifers might turn back to the spring.

Cisco was reluctant to leave but he obeyed Anatasia's shouts of "Come on, Cisco, get the cows." He hopped and barked and snapped and managed to keep going. Then, his three legs too tired, he lay down by a bush.

Anatasia was the first to miss him as they proceeded. Sancho was glad to stop while Anatasia and Amy called.

"We have to go back after him," Anatasia decided.

"How can we ever see him in all this smoke?" Amy felt without hope about anything.

"We'll keep calling. He'll hear us and try to come, or he'll bark."

"How can anyone hear anything?"

It took the persistent drumming of four heels on his sides to make Sancho move in what he knew to be an extremely unwise direction.

"Cisco won't lie somewhere and let himself burn up," Amy shouted

222

into Anatasia's ear.

"If his legs have given out he can't go, and that's all there is to it."

Amy agreed. She knew that they couldn't desert Cisco. His way of traveling—hopping instead of walking or trotting or running, as any ordinary dog would do—was exhausting on a long trip. And Cisco had worked hard helping to get the cattle moving.

They shouted and called until their throats ached. There was not much fresh air to breathe, there was too much smoke.

"Sure he can't be very far back," Anatasia said, but not hopefully. "What's that? Cisco?

But it was a lean coyote loping through the smoke.

Anatasia seized upon a new worry. "The fawn! Bucky! I don't remember seeing him much beyond the spring. Did you?"

They began calling for Bucky as well as Cisco, but the canyon had become even louder with sounds of crackling and roaring.

"Fire's getting nearer!" Anatasia yelled, urging Sancho to move faster.

29

Because it was Sunday, their day off, scarcely any of the men were on the ranch. Mr. Richie was there, however, and so were Frank and Amy's father.

When he had been out hunting the day before, Mr. Richie had observed that there were cattle near the point above the big canyon. Now, when he saw the smoke, he wanted to make sure that no cattle were trapped there. He found Amy's father and Frank by the barn, saddling horses, both in a hurry to find their children.

Mr. Richie caught a horse, flung on a saddle, and the three men started down the canyon. There, where the wind hadn't blown the dust too badly, they saw the burro's tracks.

"I'll never know why those kids took off in such a hurry," said Amy's father. "Unless it was to get to where they could watch the fire."

No one answered him. Presently, Mr. Richie said, "Further down we'll hit a trail that goes up to the ridge. We'll ride up there and see where that bunch of cattle is. If they get out on the point they'll just stand there, or jump over the cliff. Anyway, it's bad. They aren't insured against fire."

"We could lose them easy enough," Frank worried. "It's bad with this wind and the brush dry like kindling."

"Hey, listen," said Amy's father, and pulled in his horse.

Around a bend of the trail appeared the anxious white faces of cattle, cattle moving at a high trot, looking neither to the left nor the right. The men pulled off the trail and stared at the intent, hurrying animals. They trotted along, tired and frightened, heads low, saliva dripping from their mouths.

"Gee, golly," exclaimed Frank. "First time I ever seen this. Like they're being driven."

"They are," said Amy's father.

Mr. Richie said nothing. He was too busy staring at the strange assortment of ragged children, dogs and horses that now came into view.

The children stopped where they were. Dark eyes stared at Mr. Richie in dismay.

"Oh, by golly, there's your mare, Mr. Richie," Frank cried, peering, only slightly puzzled, at what was left of Mia's white markings. "Hey, Kiko, what you doing riding that mare?"

Mr. Richie had a strange feeling. There was something almost threatening about all these dark-skinned children. They were armed with sticks and clubs, and, as Frank spoke, they seemed to gather themselves defensively around the boy on the tall mare.

"And that big colt," demanded Frank. "Where'd he come from?"

"But where's Amy?" shouted Jeff Fairfield. "Where's my daughter?"

Kiko said, "Her and Anatasia must have gone back to find Cisco."

"Back there? Oh!"

"We'll find them," Frank promised, and began shouting orders as if he owned the ranch. "Mr. Richie, you get these kids and the cattle up top. Me and Mr. Fairfield are going after those girls. You watch out for this bunch of kids!" And he was off, pounding down the canyon with Amy's father riding hard at his heels.

Fire had got into the tops of some of the taller oaks, and the trees were screaming. Jeffrie Fairfield tried to pray, but everything was going so fast he could think of no words. "Help!" he gasped, to the elements and the universe in general.

Before they neared the spring, Anatasia and Amy almost rode past Cisco, who had whimpered unheard. Then he thumped his tail and Anatasia glimpsed the motion.

"Cisco, come! Oh! Where's Bucky?"

But Cisco couldn't come. He couldn't even stand up. He had overworked his muscles, he had been in cold water, he had lain down, and now he had stiffened and could travel no further. The strain on his one front leg had been too much.

Anatasia jumped off the burro, prodded and pushed to get Cisco up, but all the dog could do was to roll his eyes, whimper, wag his tail, and lick Anatasia's face.

"We got to get him up on Sancho. Help me. Let's get Sancho down in the creek bed. Then we'll drag Cisco onto his back and you can hold him on."

Amy shrieked, "Oh, hurry! The fire's coming!"

To hurry was difficult. Cisco was heavy. Sancho was too worried to want to stand quietly, but he cooperated as best he could and, with much pulling and shoving, they got Cisco across his back. Cisco lay limply and gratefully, two legs and his tail dangling down one side of Sancho, one paw and his head dangling down the other. He continued to roll his eyes and whimper, ashamed of himself to be so helpless.

"You walk beside and hold him on, I'll lead." Anatasia started off briskly. Sancho, glad to be going in the right direction at last, trotted.

Ahead of them they heard a crash that was like an extra-loud explosion. A burning oak flung itself across the canyon floor and sparks flew into the brush. Amy screamed. Sancho jumped and Cisco nearly fell off. The brush flared into a million torches.

"Holy Mother! We'll never make it!"

"Which way can we go?" Amy shouted, seeing no safe direction. Flames were rising high and red from the newly ignited brush. Wind blew sparks down canyon. The whole area would soon be ablaze.

"I know!" cried Anatasia, and swung Sancho around. She tried to run, leading him. "Get behind and hit him hard. If Cisco falls off, drag him. We got to get to the spring! Back down the canyon! Hurry!"

"But there's fire in the way!"

227

Already clumps of brush between them and the spring were flaming up. But here the brush was not a solid stand and through the smoke Anatasia tried to see ways of getting around. Both breathing and hurrying were difficult.

Suddenly Sancho seemed to agree that the spring was the best place to be, and he moved into such a fast jog that Amy, reaching out to whack him, grabbed his tail instead and that helped her along. Cisco bobbed up and down and knew he must stay on.

Anatasia swatted out a spark that landed on the front of her shirt. She ran desperately. Flames reached for them. They were all gasping and coughing, even Sancho, as they reached the small muddy clearing by the trough.

Anatasia tried to yell, "There's Bucky!" but could make no sound.

Bucky was not alone. Lying in the muddy overflow were two coyotes. Near them crouched some brush rabbits. Two does, a buck, and a fawn the size of Bucky looked at the intruders but did not run. Suddenly a gray fox appeared. Then came a little spotted skunk.

"Jump into the watering trough," Anatasia ordered Amy, as she pulled Cisco off Sancho and dumped him into the water. She dove in, soaked water into her garments, scrambled out, removed her dripping shirt and splashed Sancho all over. Then she sozzled Bucky, who didn't seem to mind in the least. She picked up an exhausted young rabbit that had just appeared, dunked him in the water and then sat him gently in the mud. The animals by the spring eyed her in mild alarm but were more frightened of the fire than of the two humans.

Amy sat up in the watering trough and peered through the smoke. The vicinity of the spring was clear of brush and dry grass, much of the earth was muddy from the overflow. She choked with smoke and felt the fire's heat on her wet face. So far as she could see in any direction, there was nothing but fire and it made the most appalling sounds.

Suddenly Anatasia shoved her completely under the water. When Amy surfaced, sputtering helplessly, Anatasia shouted, "Got to keep your hair wet. Sparks fly. Cover your nose and mouth." She produced a soggy bandana from her pocket, submerged it, then tied it firmly beneath Amy's eyes.

She bent over and plunged her own head under water. Then she turned to Cisco whose head was the only visible part of him, and held him under a second. She got her shirt dripping again and went to work on Sancho and Bucky. Sancho was shaking with his instinctive fear of fire.

Amy took off her own wet shirt and helped to get Sancho soaked, though Anatasia kept yelling at her to stay safely in the water.

"But it's safe here, isn't it?" Amy screamed.

"Unless a tree comes down on us! We better pray," and, as her mother would have her do, Anatasia knelt, made the sign of the cross, and implored Our Lord and all the saints in heaven to keep certain trees standing.

All that Amy could think to do in the way of prayer was to beg that Mia and Tesoro be kept safe somehow. She felt that she and Anatasia and the animals were in a good place. This spring where long ago the wild black horse had come to drink had become their refuge and it couldn't let harm come to them now. Not that she wasn't

229

frightened. But even in her terror she felt a security in this once-familiar spot, though now it looked so strange and unreal, like a scene from a horror movie.

The sycamore tree with its bare white trunk moved with the turmoil of wind and flame but stood firm. A scrub oak near it appeared to explode into fire. Flames rushed through the tops of trees overhead. Then a new danger appeared. Fiery branches, wind driven, came rushing along.

"Oh, watch out!" Anatasia cried despairingly.

Then, almost suddenly, the sounds of roaring, screaming, shrieking grew less. The fire had consumed all that it could in the vicinity of the spring and was surging up the brushy west side of the canyon. The black, ash-covered earth kept smoking and skeletons of trees held up smouldering branches. Everywhere the desolation was complete.

"Unless the wind changes we're safe now," Anatasia gasped thankfully.

"How will we ever get home? The ground's fiery hot."

"We'll have to wait. Wet your shirt good some more before you put it on, sparks can still be flying. I'll wet Sancho and Bucky before I put mine back on. The fire won't come back to where it's already burned, but if the wind would change it could turn and go up the canyon. But here is the safest spot in the world."

"I think the wild black horse was hiding here, too, with us. Even if we couldn't see him."

Anatasia said, "I'd rather he was near Tesoro somewhere. Keeping him from Mr. Richie."

"Well, anyway, Mia and Tesoro must be safe from the fire."

230

"But Mr. Richie!"

"We've got to get home and find out what's happening."

"We can't yet. Look. The deer and coyotes and things aren't going now. They don't want to burn their feet. When they start to go away we can start too."

"But they're looking around as if they're almost ready," Amy observed. For the first time she began to notice the wild animals with interest. She had been too terrified before, and there had been too much smoke for good viewing.

She spoke to them and they seemed to listen. "We wouldn't hurt you. Some people would, but we wouldn't."

Bucky, the pet fawn, looked at his wild cousins without much interest. He didn't know that he was a deer, he knew only that he was someone to whom Anatasia belonged. Now he stayed close by her.

Anatasia laughed for the first time that day. "Those deer must wonder why Bucky likes us so much."

30

THE BIG OAK that had crashed across the canyon floor had been an
ancient patriarch. It had stood for hundreds of years. A century ago
a fire had burned and damaged it, but it had recovered as many big
oaks do. Lightning had scarred it and it had survived that, too, but
the scars left by the old fire and by the lightning had weakened it.
Now its time had come and down it went.

It blocked the trail and set off more fire just before Frank and
Jeff Fairfield might have caught up with the girls. Their horses
whirled and bolted and when they got them stopped and turned
to look, all that they could see was fire, like a wall, between them

and where the two children might be.

"By golly, this is bad," said Frank, taking off his hat and mopping sweat and ashes from his eyes.

Under smudges of smoke Mr. Fairfield's face had turned white. He was shaking. "How can they survive?"

Frank tried to be reassuring. "That Anatasia, she knows how to take care of herself and your girl, too. They could have got into some cave in the rocks. Or found a safe clearing. Maybe by the spring."

Amy's father shook his head despairingly. "Other trees must be going down. I don't think those children have a chance. Not in *that!*"

Frank looked at the brushy hillside to the west. It too would soon be afire. "If we could circle around up there—but horses can't move fast in brush that thick."

"Let's try."

"Wait! It's already caught. We can't go that way." He looked in the other direction where the fire had moved down the east side. "Still smouldering and hot. We'll get scorched some."

It was a ride Amy's father would remember forever. In their hearts the horses were as unwilling as could be, but they were so well trained and so obedient that they did not hesitate. They jumped smouldering logs, they climbed up and slid down hot, ashy banks. Frank searched for slight clearings that the fire had missed, somehow got from clearing to clearing and found rocky ledges for hoofs to stand on.

"There!" he shouted triumphantly, and pointed to a spot on the canyon floor. Mr. Fairfield peered through veils of smoke. He saw an assortment of animals and two children moving about near a watering trough. He tried to shout but his mouth was too dry. He felt himself growing dizzy and Frank reached out to hold him in the saddle.

"Watch it! You nearly passed out. By golly, they're all right!" And he shouted above the sound of wind, "Anatasia! You kids okay?"

At first the girls couldn't tell where the shout came from. Finally they looked up, called something, and waved.

"By golly, they're okay! Like I told you, Mr. Fairfield. That Anatasia, she can look after things. Now we got to find a way to them. We can't cut straight down here, we got to circle back, I guess."

They could ride more slowly now, though for the sake of shod hoofs in hot ashes, they didn't linger. Jeff Fairfield, overcome with relief, felt weak enough to slide out of the saddle. He had never been so thankful about anything in his life; he had never been so frightened.

When they reached the spring the girls, hoping that they could soon start home, had Cisco back on Sancho, had all the animals and themselves wet again. The deer, coyotes, rabbits, fox and skunk were still there. They moved about, looking restless. The deer went bounding off as the riders approached.

Amy's father reached down, grabbed his daughter, and swung her across the saddle before him. It had been hard enough trying to breathe the thick, smoky air. Now her father's arms were so tight around her that Amy could only gasp and squirm.

She kicked. "Let me down!" she demanded when she could talk. "I have to help hold Cisco on."

Her father held her tighter. "No, we still have to hurry. Wind might change. The upper part of the canyon might catch."

Frank said, "Turn the burro loose. He'll go home safe enough.

234

Anatasia, you ride with me. We can make better time."

"But Cisco can't walk. He's got to ride Sancho."

Frank solved that. He leaped from his horse, pulled Cisco from Sancho, and thrust him into Amy's arms.

"Hang on to him somehow!"

"Our horse is overflowing already," protested Amy's father, laughing in his relief that Amy was safe. "And now here's a wet dog." But the good quarter horse didn't object. He managed his burden of man, child, and dog without showing concern.

"He'll slip off," Amy worried. "He's hard to hold and there isn't enough room."

"We'll pick him up again. We can take turns carrying him." Frank removed Sancho's rope and told the burro to go on home. Sancho was content to be free of riders, to follow the horses. Anatasia called the fawn and he came, stepping gingerly and sometimes jumping.

They had to circle and scramble up the canyon side to get around the great fallen tree. It was still burning. Cisco slid precariously this way and that but Amy managed to keep him on.

When at last they left the scorched earth and found unburned land beneath them, they felt like shouting with joy. How green the old oaks looked, how sparkling gold the dry grass!

Just before they reached the trail that would take them up the hill to the canyon's rim they met a hurrying horse and rider.

"Rudie! Comanche!" shouted Anatasia. "What happened? Where's the mare and colt?"

"In the corral by the barn," Rudie answered. "Me and the others tried to come back and find you but Mr. Richie wouldn't let us. All the kids are in Mr. Richie's office. Guess he was getting nervous on account of he sent me to see if you were in sight. He wants to see everybody right away."

"I want to go home!" Anatasia's voice was a wail. "Mama and Papa must be trying to save our house and worrying about us kids."

"Fire must be about there by now," Rudie said. "It must have got all that mountain where Mia—" He stopped, confused, hesitant to mention Mia in front of his Uncle Frank. He said brightly, "But I bet the fire break they made must have slowed it down on the reservation."

Neither Frank nor Amy's father answered him.

When they reached the safety of the upper cleared land the air was heavy with moving smoke and they could see the progress of the fire, off to the southwest. A forestry truck went rushing along one of the ranch roads.

"Look!" cried Rudie. "I bet they started a backfire on the reservation. They made a fire break and then they burned on the other side. You can tell! See where that new smoke comes up? I bet we're safe over there now."

"When the wind drops," Frank said, "they'll get it out with those fire bombers dropping that stuff."

But Anatasia and Rudie and Amy had ceased to think about the fire. They worried steadily about Mia and Tesoro, about what Mr. Richie would do. When they reached the barn they all slid off and hurried toward Mr. Richie's office.

"Hey, Amy, no!" shouted her father. "I'm taking you home."

"No!" shouted Amy, above the wind's screaming. "No, I have to see about things."

Just then Amy's mother drove up. She jammed on her brakes.

"Amy! Oh, thank heaven!" she cried. Poor Mrs. Fairfield had been wildly driving along what ranch roads were open, desperately searching for her daughter.

"Oh, Amy! Come home this minute!" she commanded.

But Amy was going through the office door which Mr. Richie, who was standing there like a guard, opened for her.

31

THE ROOM WAS crowded with children. The dogs, shut outside, whined as did the wind at the door. The fawn had pushed his way in and now lay wearily at Anatasia's feet.

Amy was glad that her father and mother were there beside her for the time of reckoning had come. She was very nearly too tired to think of what Mr. Richie would say. Instead, she thought with sadness that by now the fire must have roared through their spot on the mountain, that it would be a long time before it would be beautiful again. She hoped that the Indians had saved their homes on the reservation.

238

Frank was there, sitting straight beside Kiko, and Anatasia and her brothers had crowded close to Kiko as if for reassurance.

When Mr. Richie cleared his throat and stared at them, Amy could see that he was almost too angry to speak. When at last he did begin to talk his voice cut through the room like a knife. Amy felt stung by the harsh rasp of his words.

"I want a full explanation!"

Only the wind replied, howling dismally as it brought the bitter smell of smoke into the room.

"Well? Somebody speak up. One of you—*talk!*" Mr. Richie commanded.

Amy took a quivering breath. "We saved their lives. Mia's and the colt's.

Mr. Richie stared at her, uncomprehending.

"You'd have killed the colt and perhaps Mia, too, if she hadn't done well," Amy continued rapidly.

"And how did you know about that?" Mr. Richie's voice was as cold as his eyes.

Amy fought back. "Kiko told me. The colt couldn't be left to live because you'd think he was a scrub colt and a disgrace to your ranch. So we hid Mia and raised the colt. *We had to!*"

Amy's father was shaking his head in bewilderment. "You children—so *that's* what you've been up to!"

But all eyes were focused on Mr. Richie. Not a child in the room stirred. For several moments Mr. Richie did not speak but his look held them silent and scared.

"What you have done is criminal," he said at last. "You dared to take things into your own hands. This is my ranch. I've spent a lifetime building up a line of blooded stock. I can't jeopardize my reputation and that of this ranch by raising a scrub half-breed. But you dared to do that to me. If you were older I'd have you jailed."

In the silence that followed Frank, unexpectedly bold, spoke up. "It's a good colt, Mr. Richie," he said softly.

His words gave Amy courage. "He *is* a good colt! Please just look at him, Mr. Richie," she pleaded. "Just *see* him. He's like the wild black Thoroughbred used to be. He was the colt's ancestor. Tesoro is a throw-back."

Then, in spite of her fear, Amy began to tell about the hide-away on the mountain, about the colt's birth, about getting feed for them, and about Kiko training Mia.

Her father kept right on shaking his head and looking surprised. "You kids—I can't believe it," he kept saying. Amy took heart. He didn't seem angry.

She thought that Frank was beginning to look secretly pleased. "Golly!" he said several times. "You didn't have no help—from nobody?"

"Not until later," Amy answered him. "Anatasia saved us from Mr. Bashford and we needed her and the twins for when school started. Then, when the fire came, all the Indian kids and their dogs hurried to help."

Mr. Richie had remained silent throughout Amy's account. Now he broke in, and his words, spoken curtly, his hard voice level and dry, brought them abruptly back to the present painful moment. "It's quite a story, I'll admit. But stealing a mare is a serious thing. Don't any of you realize that you can be in a great deal of trouble? What if I call the sheriff?"

240

"But we *didn't* steal!" Amy protested, fighting for them all. "We only saved. Soon we were going to take Mia back to the home pasture. We had a plan. About Tesoro—"

"You don't seem to understand what stealing is," barked Mr. Richie. "Saving a horse, having plans—especially with Indians—that's less than an excuse."

Amy's father interrupted. He looked directly at Mr. Richie but he spoke to Frank. "Frank," he said, "did you count how many head of big heifers the kids saved from the fire?"

"Sure, I counted them, Mr. Fairfield. Twenty-one head." Frank was beginning to grin.

"That's what I made it. Now, Frank, if you said that they're worth roughly a hundred dollars a head—and they're worth more, undoubtedly—what would that come to?"

"Golly! Let's see now. Would that be twenty-one hunderd dollars? That's two thousand and one hunderd dollars."

Mr. Fairfield shifted his gaze to Amy. "When you kids went after those heifers you must have known that someone might come riding, that the mare and the colt would be discovered. You did know that, didn't you?"

Amy nodded. "But we had to. The fire was coming fast toward that point. We didn't even think. We just hurried because Kiko said to."

Her father turned back to Mr. Richie. "Now that you think it over, are you so sure these kids are criminals? Are you so certain that 'saving,' as Amy called it, is the same as 'stealing'?"

Mr. Richie's face did not change expression but he seemed to be considering Jeff Fairfield's words. He looked around the room at the dark-skinned, dark-eyed, smoke-smudged children.

"These children did something they shouldn't have done. No matter what their reasons, I can't approve their actions. Furthermore, they endangered themselves and me by wanting to run back into the fire to find a dog and a fawn and a burro and two other children. Bringing them up out of the canyon wasn't easy."

He paused. Then Amy thought she saw a flicker of grudging admiration in his stern expression—a brief flicker that changed to puzzlement—and Amy didn't know that at the moment Mr. Richie was taking a quick look into himself.

"You kids," he said slowly. "You crazy kids—"

Mrs. Fairfield looked at him brightly and spoke for the first time. "See?" she said.

"What about it, Richie?" Mr. Fairfield asked.

Mr. Richie moved a little uneasily. He very nearly smiled. "You can have the colt," he said to the children. "But take him to the reservation and keep him there, if you value him!"

The room was silent as every child seemed to be holding his breath.

"And the mare?" persisted Amy's father.

"That's another matter," answered Mr. Richie.

"Two thousand and one hundred dollars. That's a great deal of money," said Mr. Fairfield, giving no inch. "If you count the future worth of those heifers and the calves they'll have, there's more money than that involved. Much more."

Mr. Richie suddenly stood up and, as he did so, something terrible seemed to fall away. The room seemed lighter. "I'll think about the mare," said Mr. Richie. "Had enough of this. Got to see what they're doing on the fire line. Consider yourselves lucky, kids, that the sheriff won't be told." At the door he paused. "Hey—don't just sit there! You'd better go out and rub that mare down. And walk her. She's hot. What's wrong with you kids? Do you want her to stiffen up in this wind?"

And then Mr. Richie was out the door and gone. And Amy and Kiko smiled. Everybody smiled.

J   05336

Van der Veer
  Hold the rein free